THE GOLDEN TOWER

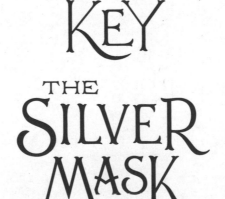

MAGISTERIUM

BOOK FIVE

THE GOLDEN TOWER

HOLLY BLACK *and* CASSANDRA CLARE

WITH ILLUSTRATIONS BY
SCOTT FISCHER

SCHOLASTIC PRESS / NEW YORK

Library of Congress Cataloging-in-Publication Data available

ISBN 978-0-545-52240-3

10 9 8 7 6 5 4 3 2 1   18 19 20 21 22

Printed in the U.S.A.   23
First edition, September 2018

Book design by Christopher Stengel

FOR CAMMIE AND ELLIOT,
WHO ARE BOTH GOOD AT BEING BAD.

↑ ≈ △○◉

CHAPTER ONE

FOR THE FIRST time in Call's life, the house he had grown up in looked small.

Alastair brought the car to a stop and they piled out along with Havoc, who ran along the edge of the grass, barking. Alastair glanced at Call once before locking the car — there was no suitcase to carry out, no duffel bags or luggage to worry about. Call had come home from Master Joseph's with nothing.

Not exactly nothing, said Aaron's voice in his head. *You've got me.*

Call tried not to smile. It would be weird if his dad saw him grinning at nothing, especially since lately there hadn't been much to smile about — Master Joseph and his forces had been defeated by the Magisterium, but there had been a high death toll. Call's best friend, Aaron, had been raised from the dead only to die again.

As far as anyone knew.

"Are you all right?" Alastair squinted at Call. "You look dyspeptic."

Call abandoned the attempt not to smile. "Just glad to be home."

Alastair hugged him awkwardly. "I don't blame you."

The house looked smaller inside, too. Call went into his bedroom, Havoc panting at his heels. It was still weird to see Havoc with regular green wolf eyes instead of the coruscating eyes of the Chaos-ridden. Call reached down to scratch Havoc's ears and the wolf yawned, his tail thumping on the ground.

Call wandered around the room, picking things up almost aimlessly and putting them down. His old Iron Year uniform. Smooth, pebbled rocks from the caverns of the Magisterium. A picture of him and Aaron and Tamara, grinning ear to ear.

Tamara. His stomach clenched.

He hadn't spoken to Tamara since she had been kneeling over his body on the battlefield outside Master Joseph's stronghold. In that moment, it had seemed possible that she cared about him the way he wanted her to, but the silence that followed let him know where he stood. After all, it was one thing to not want someone to die; it was another thing entirely to want to talk to them once they were alive.

Tamara hadn't wanted Call to raise Aaron from the dead in the first place, and once he had, she hadn't thought that

Aaron was himself. To be fair, Aaron *hadn't* been acting like himself. It turned out that bringing a soul back into a slightly rotted body did weird things to it. Ironically, Aaron was much more himself now while rattling around in Call's head. But Tamara didn't know Aaron was still around, and Call was sure, based on her previous reactions, that she would be highly suspicious if she found out. She already thought Call was an evil sorcerer, or at least evilly inclined.

Which Call didn't really want to think about, because of all the people in the world, Tamara had always believed in him the most.

We're still going to have to tell her, you know.

Call startled. Despite Aaron being there with him in the Magisterium infirmary all through his healing from the after-effects of using too much chaos magic at the battle with Alex, another person hearing and responding to your thoughts never stopped being unsettling.

There was a knock on the door and then Alastair opened it. "You feel up to some dinner? I could make some grilled pimento cheese sandwiches. Or we could get a pizza."

"Sandwiches would be great," Call said.

Alastair made them carefully, buttering up the pan so the bread got nicely toasted and opening a can of tomato soup. Call's dad had never been much of a cook, but eating dinner at the table with him — and sneaking crusts to Havoc under the table — was way better than the most delicious feast Master Joseph could conjure.

"So," Alastair started, once he'd sat down and they'd both started eating. The tomato soup was salty-sweet, just right, and the pimento cheese perfectly spicy. "We need to talk about the future."

Call looked up from his soup, puzzled. "Future?"

"You're heading into your Gold Year at the Magisterium. Everyone agrees that you've, um, learned enough magic for your Silver Year to be considered complete. You'll be walking through the gate as soon as you get back to school in the fall."

"I can't go back to the Magisterium!" Call said. "Everyone hates me."

Alastair pushed back his dark hair absently. "Probably not so much anymore. You're a hero again." Call's dad was a great dad in many ways, but his bedside manner still needed a lot of work. "Anyway, you only have to make it through one more year of study. And with Master Joseph gone, it ought to be pretty quiet."

"The Collegium —"

"You don't have to go to the Collegium, Call," Alastair said. "And I think it would be better if you didn't. Now that Aaron's gone, you're the only Makar left. They'll try to use you, and they'll never trust you. You can't have a normal mage's life."

Call thought privately he wasn't sure any mage had a normal life. "Then what'll I do instead? Go to regular college?"

"I never went to any kind of college," said Alastair. "We could take some time off, travel a little. I could teach you what

I do — we could set up a business somewhere, father and son.
Like California." He poked his soup with his spoon. "I mean,
we'll have to change our names. Avoid the Magisterium and
the Assembly. But it's worth it."

Call didn't know what to say. Right now the idea of never
dealing with the Assembly and its views on Makars, or the
hatred people held toward Constantine Madden, the Enemy of
Death, whose soul lived in Call's body, sounded ideal. But . . .

"Look, there's something I've got to tell you," Call said.
"Aaron's not really gone."

Alastair's brows furrowed in concern.

Uh-oh, Aaron thought. *I hope he's not going to freak out.*

"What do you mean?" Alastair said carefully.

"I mean, he's still in my head. Like, he's living on in me,"
Call blurted out.

There's really no need for you to tell him this, Aaron said.
Which was pretty rich coming from him, since he'd just gotten through saying they had to tell Tamara.

Alastair nodded slowly, and relief made Call's shoulders
dip. His dad was taking this well. Maybe he'd have some ideas
for what to do.

"That's a good way of looking at it," Alastair said finally.
"You're dealing with all of this really well. Grief is hard, I
know. But the best thing to do is to remember the person you
lost and —"

"You don't understand," Call interrupted. "Aaron talks to
me. I *hear* him."

Alastair continued nodding. "I felt that way sometimes after we lost your mother. It was almost as though I could hear Sarah's voice scolding me. Especially one time when I let you crawl around outside and you ate dirt while I wasn't paying attention."

"I ate dirt?" Call asked.

"Helps you build immunities," said Alastair, slightly defensive. "You're fine."

"I might be," said Call. "But that's not the point. The point is that Aaron is really, really with me."

Alastair put a gentle hand on Call's shoulder. "I know he is," he said.

And Call didn't have the heart to say anything after that.

↑ ≈ △ ○ @

The night before leaving home for his final year at the Magisterium, Call lay awake in bed as the moon made a white path over his bedclothes. He had packed a duffel for his trip to the Magisterium the next day, where he'd be putting on the deep red uniform of a Gold Year. He remembered looking at Alex Strike in his Gold Year uniform, seeming so cool and confident with his friends. Now Alex was dead. Call was glad, too. Alex had murdered Aaron and deserved everything he'd gotten.

Call. Aaron's voice was a whisper. *Don't think about this stuff. You just have to get through tomorrow.*

"But everyone will hate me," Call said. He knew his father disagreed, but he was pretty sure he was right about this. He might have come out on the right side in the last battle, he might have saved the Magisterium, but he was still the bearer of Constantine Madden's corrupted soul.

Havoc gave a whine and nosed at Call's hand, then began trying to crawl under the covers. It had been cute when he was a pup but was downright dangerous in a full-grown wolf, even if he wasn't Chaos ridden.

Havoc, quit it, Aaron thought, and Havoc jerked his head up, blinking. *He can hear me!* Aaron sounded delighted.

"You're imagining things," Call said.

There was a knock on Call's door. "Call? Are you on the phone?" Alastair asked.

"No!" Call yelled. "Just — talking to Havoc."

"Okay." Alastair sounded dubious but his footsteps receded.

You've got Tamara, and Havoc, and me, said Aaron. *As long as we all stick together, we'll be all right.*

CHAPTER TWO

S ITTING ON THE passenger side of Alastair's silver 1937 Rolls-Royce Phantom, headed toward the Magisterium once again, Call thought about his trip to the Iron Trial four years earlier. He remembered the way his dad had told him that, if he just flunked the tests, then he wouldn't have to go to magic school — which was good, because if he did go, he might die down in the tunnels.

Now Call knew what his dad had really been worried about — the discovery that Call was the repository for Constantine's soul. And everything his dad had been afraid might happen had come to pass, except for the dying-in-the-tunnels part.

It wasn't too late for that either.

Do you just think about the worst stuff possible? Aaron asked. *Like this Evil Overlord point system. We really need to talk about that.*

"Don't judge," Call said.

Alastair looked over at him oddly. "I am not judging you, Callum. Although you have been very quiet on this trip."

Call really needed to stop responding to Aaron out loud.

And Aaron really needed to stop poking around in his memories.

"I'm fine," Call told his dad. "Just a little on edge."

"Only one more year," said Alastair, turning onto the road that led to the caverns of the school. "And then the mages can't claim you're dangerously untrained or any of that hogwash. One more year and you'll be free from mages forever."

A few minutes later, Call was getting out of the car and slinging a duffel over his shoulder. Havoc jumped out after him, scenting the wind. A bus was letting out other students, young ones fresh from the Iron Trials. They looked really small to Call and he found himself worrying for them. A few peered over at him nervously, pointing and whispering to one another.

He stopped worrying and started hoping Warren, a weird lizard that lived in the caves, would lead them into a crevasse.

That would definitely earn you some of those Evil Overlord Points, Aaron said.

"Stop poking around in my brain," Call muttered under his breath.

Alastair came around and gave him a parting hug and a

pat on the shoulder. With a start, Call realized they were basically the same height now.

He could hear whispers all around them, was conscious of eyes staring at him and his father. When Alastair stepped back, his jaw was tight. "You're a good kid," he said. "They don't deserve you."

With a sigh, Call watched him drive away, then made his way into the caves of the Magisterium. Havoc padded along behind him.

Everything felt familiar and not familiar. The scent of stone, intensifying as he wended his way deeper into the maze of tunnels, was familiar. The sound of small scuttling lizards and the glow of the moss was familiar. The way the other students stared at him and whispered behind their hands was familiar, too, but much less pleasant. Even some of the Masters were doing it. Call caught Master Rockmaple gaping at him as he approached the door to his rooms, and made a face right back.

He tapped his wristband against the door and it popped open. He ducked in, expecting the room to be empty.

It wasn't. Tamara was sitting on the couch, already in her Gold Year uniform.

Why did you think she wouldn't be here? Aaron asked him. *It's her room, too.*

For once, Call didn't answer Aaron out loud, but that was only because there was a roaring in his ears and all he could think about was Tamara. About how pretty she looked and how shiny her hair was, braided in one heavy plait, and how everything about her seemed perfectly ordered, from the sharpness of her brows to the spotlessness of her uniform.

That was weird, Aaron said. *Your whole mind just went up in smoke or something. Call? Earth to Call?*

He had to say something. He knew he had to say something, especially because she was still looking at him, like she was waiting for him to do exactly that.

But he felt shabby and awkward and completely foolish. And he didn't know how he was going to explain that he maybe hadn't made all the right choices, but they'd worked out in the end and he wasn't mad at her for running off with Jasper and leaving him at Evil Overlord Central with Master Joseph and Alex so she probably shouldn't be mad at him for raising Aaron from the dead. . . .

Nope, you can't say any of that, Aaron said firmly.

"Why?" Call asked, and then realized he'd done it again, he'd spoken out loud. He resisted slapping his hand over his mouth, which would only make things worse.

Tamara stood up from the couch. "*Why?* That's all you've got to say to me?"

"No!" Call said, but then realized he hadn't worked out what he *should* say.

Repeat after me, said Aaron. "*Tamara, I know you've got reasons to be mad and I know I've got to regain your trust, but I hope we can be friends again one day.*"

Call took a deep breath. "I know you've got reasons to be mad," he said, feeling even more foolish, if that were possible.

"And I know I've got to regain your trust, but I hope we can be friends again one day."

Tamara's expression softened. "We can be friends, Call."

Call couldn't believe what he'd said had worked. Aaron always knew what to say, and now, with Aaron in his head, Call would know what to say, too! That was great.

"Okay," he said now, since he wasn't receiving any other instructions. "Good."

Tamara bent down and ruffled the fur around Havoc's throat, making the wolf's tongue loll with happiness. "He really seems fine, not being Chaos-ridden. He doesn't even seem that different."

Now tell her that you care about her and you've made some bad choices and you're sorry about them, Aaron told him.

I am not going to say that! Call thought back. *If I tell her I care about her, she'll laugh at me. But if I don't say anything else, maybe this will all blow over.*

All he got from Aaron in return was silence. Sulky silence.

"I care about you," Call said, and Tamara stood bolt upright. Both she and Havoc looked at him in surprise. "I made bad choices. Really bad choices. Like, the worst choices anyone has ever made."

Don't go overboard, buddy. Aaron sounded alarmed.

"I wanted Aaron back," Call said, and Aaron, in his head, was silent. "You and Aaron — you're the best friends I've ever had. And Havoc. But he doesn't judge."

Havoc barked. Tamara's lip twitched a little, as if she was trying not to smile.

"I don't want to pressure you," Call said. "Take all the time you need to decide how you feel. I just wanted you to know I was sorry."

Tamara was silent for a long moment. Then she walked over to him and kissed him on the cheek. Energy zinged through Call's body and he fought off the urge to put his arms around her.

Yikes, Aaron said mildly.

Tamara pulled back. "That doesn't mean I totally forgive you or we're back to where we were," she said. "We're not dating, Call."

"I know," Call said. He hadn't expected anything else, but it still felt like a dull thump to the chest.

"But we *are* friends," she said. Her eyes sparkled fiercely. "Look, everyone here believes something different about you now. They don't know anything about how you — about Aaron being raised. They know Master Joseph kidnapped you, and they know you helped defeat him and Alex."

"Good?" Call said cautiously. "That seems . . . good?"

"But they all know you have the soul of the Enemy of Death now. Everyone knows it, Call. I don't know how much they're going to be able to understand that you're *not* him."

"I could just stay in this room all year." Call glanced around. "I can get food by enchanting bologna the way Master Rufus did when we first arrived."

Tamara shook her head. "No way. First of all, we don't have any bologna. Second, we're going to go out there and face them. You need to be able to have a normal life as a mage, Call. You have to show everyone that you're just you, that you're not some monster."

I might never have a life as a mage, Call thought. *This might be it.*

Aaron, in his head, remained silent. Call was pretty sure he shouldn't say anything to Tamara about his father's suggestion to skip the Collegium and run out on the mage world altogether. He was too confused about it himself.

"Okay," he said. "I'm in. What do you want to do first? Go to the Gallery?"

"First, I have something to give you," Tamara said, surprising him. She went into her room, her braid swinging, and came out carrying — a knife. *Call's* knife, made by his mother, the hilt and scabbard decorated with swirling patterns.

"Miri," he breathed, taking the weapon back. "Tamara — thank you."

Now, if anyone in the Refectory bothers you, you can chop off their head, Aaron thought cheerfully.

Call started to choke, but luckily, Tamara chalked it up to emotion and patted him on the back until he stopped.

CHAPTER THREE

WALKING INTO THE Refectory gave Call a feeling not unlike déjà vu. He felt as though he was in a familiar place, but nothing quite looked right. And he realized it was because he recognized so few of the other students. All the older kids he knew were gone. He didn't know anyone in their Iron Year, barely knew anyone in Copper or Bronze Year, and even the Gold and Silver Year students he knew looked a lot different. A few had what looked like the scraggly beginnings of beards.

Call put his hand to his own face. He should have shaved this morning. Tamara would probably like that.

Focus, Aaron told him.

If Aaron were here, in a separate body, he would remember to shave. He would sculpt his facial hair with natural confidence and skill, and everyone would admire him for it.

We'll find me a body soon enough, said Aaron.

Wait. *What?* Call thought.

But before he could dwell on that more, Tamara gave him a shove toward the food. With his stomach in knots on the way to the Magisterium, he hadn't eaten very much, but having Tamara on his side made him feel so much better that he found he was starving.

He got some greenish lichen, some slices of large mushroom, and a few purple ball-like dumplings in a blue sauce.

Get some turnip cakes, Aaron said. *They're good.*

Call had never cared for the pale turnip cakes, which looked too much like they were made from eyeless fish for his taste, but he plopped a few on his plate anyway. Taking a cup of tea, he followed Tamara to a table. She found one where it was going to be just them, set down her tray, and looked around, as though daring someone to approach.

No one did. Lots of people were looking at their table and whispering, but no one was coming over.

"Hey, um, how is Kimiya?" Call asked finally, just to say something.

Tamara rolled her eyes but surprisingly also grinned. "Grounded and kept home from the Collegium for a whole year for making out with Evil Overlord Alex. Also for joining his evil army of evil."

"Wow," said Call.

He looked up to see three Iron Year kids heading toward the table. Three boys — a pale kid with white-blond hair, a darker-skinned kid with lots of curls, and another kid covered in freckles.

"Um, hi," said the pale kid. "I'm Axel. Are you really the Enemy of Death?"

"He's not the Enemy!" Tamara said.

"Well," said Call, "I have his soul, I guess. But I'm not him. You don't have to be afraid of me."

All three Iron Years had taken a step back when he'd begun talking, so he wasn't sure how convincing he'd been. They were looking at him as though waiting for him to bare his teeth, when Jasper came up behind them.

"Scram, munchkins!" Jasper yelled, causing them to yelp and run back to their table.

Jasper laughed uproariously. He had an even weirder haircut than before — somehow both spiky and shaggy at the same time — and was wearing a leather jacket over his uniform.

"That's not helpful," said Tamara. "We must reach out to them with understanding, not scare them off like they're little kids at a Halloween party."

Jasper made a face at her. "Good to see you all, too!" he said, and headed off toward Celia and the food. Call couldn't help gazing after Celia, who was wearing a headband in place of the old sparkly hair clips she'd worn when she was younger. Once, she'd been his really good friend. She'd even wanted to *date* him. Now, she wouldn't look at him.

"Hi!" Call turned to see Gwenda, tray in hand. She sat down opposite them and started eating calmly. Call looked at her in surprise. Either she was enormously out of the loop of school gossip or she didn't care about *anything.*

"What's up?" she asked.

"I'm the Enemy of Death," Call said to her, in case she hadn't heard.

She rolled her eyes. "I know. *Everyone* knows. Too bad about Alex — he was pretty hot."

"He wasn't hot, he was *evil,*" said Tamara.

"Evil, yeah. Everybody knows that, too," said Gwenda. She waved across the room. "Kai! Rafe! Over here!"

Kai and Rafe were standing over by a huge soup tureen. They looked at each other and shrugged before moving to join the table. They both nodded at Call before digging into their food.

"Jasper and Celia are back together again," Gwenda said, gesturing with her fork. Call followed her gaze and saw that Jasper and Celia had indeed taken their trays to a table by themselves and had their lips fused together like two snorklers. Jasper had his hands in Celia's blond hair.

"After the whole battle at Master Joseph's, Celia decided Jasper was a hero," said Rafe. "Instalove."

"Instabacktolove," corrected Gwenda. "Since she dumped him before that."

Soon they were all chatting about who at school had broken up or gotten together, who the new Masters were, and what movies were showing in the Gallery. Aaron stayed quiet in Call's mind, listening. It felt normal — so normal that Call started to relax.

Just then Celia pulled away from Jasper and caught Call's eye. Her look was icy. Jasper tried to draw her back, but she was on her feet, stalking over to Call's table.

"You," she snapped, pointing at him. The whole room fell silent, as if they'd been waiting for this. "You're the Enemy of Death, you *liar.*"

Tamara bolted to her feet. "Celia, you don't understand —"

"I do understand. I understand everything! He lied to all of us! Constantine Madden was sneaky and evil, and now Call has snuck back into the Magisterium and Aaron Stewart is *dead* because of him!"

It's not because of you, Aaron thought quietly. *Don't listen.*

But Call couldn't avoid listening.

"Celia," Jasper said, coming up behind her and putting his hands on her shoulders. "Celia, come on. He's more like the Frenemy of Death."

But she shook him off.

"I have family who would still be alive today if it wasn't for you," Celia said. "Constantine Madden killed them. And that means *you* killed them, just like you killed Aaron."

"I didn't kill Aaron," Call managed to say. His whole face felt hot and his heart was speeding. Everyone in the whole Refectory was looking at them.

"You might as well have!" Celia said. "The Enemy of Death's Chaos-ridden and his minions were all looking for you. They were fixated on you. You're the only reason any of them were at the Magisterium."

Miserably, Call couldn't think of anything to say to that.

It's not your fault, Aaron said, but Aaron was wrong.

"I'm sorry," Call finally replied. "I don't remember being anyone but Call, but I would do anything to have Aaron back. I would do anything for him to have not died in the first place."

Celia looked as though the wind had gone out of her sails. She looked around at the people sitting at Call's table, at Tamara. Celia's eyes got a strange shine, like maybe she was blinking back tears.

"You're trying to make me look bad, like I'm the mean one," Celia said.

"Remember how you spread rumors about Aaron?" Tamara asked. "You're not perfect, Celia."

Celia's neck flushed a painful red. "Call is the *Enemy of Death*. He's a megalomaniacal monster, but I guess because he doesn't *gossip*, it's okay."

"Call is a good person," Tamara said. "He's a hero. Because of him, the Enemy's minions are disbanded. Master Joseph is dead."

That one was me, Aaron said, which almost made Call snort with surprised laughter. If he had, the whole Magisterium might have decided Celia was right about him.

"It's a trick," Celia said. "I know it's a trick, even if you're all too stupid to see it." With that, she turned on her heel and stomped out of the Refectory.

"We're, uh, still working stuff out," Jasper said, hurrying after her.

Call stood up, not wanting to be there anymore either. Everyone was staring at him and he just wanted to go to classes and be alone with Tamara and Master Rufus. He couldn't keep on pretending everything was normal.

An announcement came echoing through the room: "All apprentices should make their way to the main entrance hall. Classes will be canceled for the first half of the day for a general assembly."

With a sinking feeling, Call was sure that this had something to do with him.

CHAPTER FOUR

STANDING IN THE great entry hall, Call remembered being there for the first time, listening to Master Rufus speak, his heart beating as hard then as it was beating now. He remembered marveling at the glittering mica floor, the flowstone walls, the enormous stalagmites and hanging stalactites, the bright glowing blue river snaking through the room, making you have to be careful where you stood, even though the place was enormous.

Back then he'd been worried about eyeless fish and getting lost in the tunnels. Now, those worries seemed to belong to a different person.

Tamara took his hand and squeezed it, surprising him.

Did that mean she still liked him? Did that mean they might get back together after all? Jasper had gotten back together with Celia and he was a pill, so maybe Call had a chance.

Celia is also a pill, Aaron said, which was mean for Aaron. *She shouldn't have said that stuff to you.*

"I thought you liked Celia," Call said, and Tamara looked at him in surprise. He'd spoken quietly, but not quietly enough.

"I do," she said. "I did. But when she says those things to you — I mean, she's insulting all of us. I know she thinks we're brainwashed minions." She flushed with anger. "Celia can go eat an eyeless fish."

More and more students were crowding into the entry hall. Call was forced to move slightly closer to Tamara, which was fine with him. "What happened to reaching out to people with understanding?"

"I took a break from it," said Tamara. "Look, Celia might come around, she's just very —"

A sound like a massive metal gong being struck rang through the room. Metal magic — Call felt Miri, strapped to his hip, vibrate in tune. There was the rush of air being displaced and suddenly Master Rufus was hovering above them all, looking down. Beside him were some other mages, familiar teachers and unfamiliar ones. Master North loomed to one side, with Master Rockmaple and Master Milagros on the other.

Call hadn't seen Master Rufus since the battlefield. A shudder went up his spine at the memory. He had been so close to dying. And even closer to losing everything that mattered to him.

"Students," Master Rufus boomed, his voice amplified by air magic. "We have called you here because we know that rumors and anxiety are running rampant among you. This is indeed a time of great instability in the magical world. Master Joseph, a minion of the Enemy of Death, tried to destroy the mage world in the name of Constantine Madden. But he was *defeated.*" The word boomed out defiantly. "We have all known people who went over to the side of the Enemy out of selfishness and out of fear."

There was a murmur. Call realized quite a few people were looking at Jasper and flashed suddenly to an almost-buried memory of an Assembly guard dragging Jasper's father away from the battlefield with his hands bound.

"Many of those mages are now in the Panopticon or being held by the Assembly. Treat those who have family members who are being rehabilitated with compassion. Their disappointment in their loved ones is already great enough."

Jasper flushed dark red and looked at the floor.

"We must learn from this lesson that we cannot allow fear to rule us," said Master Rufus. "Gossip, suspicion of your fellow apprentices — all that comes from fear. But fear has no place in a mage's heart. It was fear of death that set Constantine Madden on his path. When fear rules us, we forget who we truly are. We forget the good we are capable of."

The crowd had fallen silent.

"There are those among us who you may fear because you do not understand them," said Master Rufus. "But Callum

Hunt, our Makar, helped close this last chapter on the tragic legacy of the Enemy of Death. When it mattered, he rose up on the side of law and order, of goodness and humanity. Evil will always rise — and good will always defeat it." Rufus crossed his arms over his chest. "A round of applause for Callum Hunt."

The applause was faint. Tamara dropped Call's hand so she could clap, and slowly others joined in. It was hardly a standing ovation, but it was something. It died away quickly as Master Rufus and the other mages floated down from their high perch and stalked majestically from the room, signaling that the meeting was over.

"So . . . now what?" asked Call, hanging back as the other students filed out. He didn't want any more attention drawn to him.

Tamara shrugged. "We've got time. I guess we could go back to our room."

"Okay," Call said with mixed feelings. He wanted to be alone with Tamara, but he was also worried that maybe he didn't know what to say to her. After all, the only reason she wasn't mad at him was because of what Aaron had told him to say — and if she liked the stuff that Aaron said, maybe it was really Aaron she'd always liked. That's what Jasper had thought. That's what Call had thought, too, if he was honest with himself. Everyone liked Aaron better than Call. Why would she be any different?

She told you she likes you, Aaron said, and Call winced. He didn't mind Aaron hearing most of the stuff he thought, but he wished he could hide the thoughts he had about Aaron himself.

Well, you can't, said Aaron.

With a sigh, Call walked through the halls of the Magisterium, trying to concentrate on not thinking at all. Maybe he could take Havoc for another walk. Havoc liked walks.

As Call waved his wristband in front of the door and it slid open, he saw that Master Rufus was waiting for them. He sat on the couch, peering at Call and Tamara from beneath his bushy, expressive brows.

"Welcome back to the Magisterium," he said. "I hope you're pleased to be here."

"It's better than the Panopticon," said Call. "That was quite a speech you gave."

"Yes," said Master Rufus. "I thought so, too. I hope you're both ready for your next lesson. You might have learned enough magic to walk through the Gate of Silver, but you haven't learned the same magic as the other apprentice groups. You're going to have to hustle to catch up."

Call rolled his eyes. "Great."

Master Rufus went on, ignoring this comment. "As Tamara is well aware, there are awards given to students at the end of their Gold Year, awards that will help you toward getting ahead in the Collegium and in the mage world beyond. No time for dawdling if you'd like to win something."

"You've got to be kidding me," said Call. "Nothing I do in my Gold Year is going to keep people from thinking of me as that guy who used to be the Enemy of Death."

"Perhaps," said Master Rufus. "But what about Tamara?"

Call looked over at her guiltily. "She'll do great," he said, wanting it to be true. Thinking about Tamara not getting all the awards and prizes she deserved made him feel awful. She'd been the best at the tests in the Iron Trial. She was the best at *everything*. If she didn't win, it was because of him. No wonder he needed Aaron to tell him what to say to her.

"I'll try," said Tamara, and elbowed Call. "We both will."

Tell her you'll work as hard as you can, Aaron said.

"I'll put my best effort into it," Call said, and both Tamara and Master Rufus looked at him in surprise.

"Glad to hear it," Master Rufus said finally, rising to his feet. "Are the two of you ready to go?"

Call was startled — he hadn't realized the lesson was going to start *now*. "Guess so," he said.

It seemed to him that Tamara was looking at him strangely, but once they reached the corridor, she fell into step beside him and even bumped his shoulder with hers, so maybe he'd been imagining it. Master Rufus stalked ahead of them, cutting a swath through the crowds of students heading back from the entry hall.

"What do you think it's going to be?" Call said under his breath as Master Rufus led them into a less crowded corridor, then down a set of natural stone steps that descended into a cathedral-sized cavern. A blue underground pool glimmered in the center; Call had forgotten how weirdly beautiful the Magisterium could be. "What've I missed?"

"Everything," Tamara said, but without rancor. "Um, finer control of fire magic, storm control, weather magic, metallurgy . . ."

Call's leg had started to ache fiercely by the time they reached the pebbled floor of the cavern. He'd shattered it when he was very young and it hadn't healed right. Several surgeries later, he was sure it never would. Other students had already arrived; Call recognized Gwenda, Celia, Rafe, Kai, and Jasper, looking sullen. Master Milagros was there, too, and quickly explained that they'd be splitting into teams. She assigned Celia and Jasper to be team captains.

"Great," Call muttered to Tamara. "Now I'm never getting picked."

Celia had first choice and picked Rafe. Then it was Jasper's turn. He strode up and down the line of waiting students like a drill sergeant in a war movie inspecting uniforms. He was even squinting one eye shut and chewing an imaginary cigar, which Call felt was overkill.

"A tough choice, a tough choice," he announced finally, coming to a stop with his hands behind his back. "A lot of fine candidates."

"Jasper, get on with it," said Master Rufus. "It's one exercise, not a lifetime commitment."

Jasper sighed, as if to say *misunderstood again.* "Callum Hunt," he chose.

There was a low buzz of surprise. Even Tamara made a startled noise. Call was too puzzled to move, until Tamara poked him in the back. He went to join Jasper, all eyes on them both.

Celia was pink-cheeked with annoyance. Jasper looked at her sadly. "She doesn't understand why I picked you," he said as Call joined him.

"Neither do I," said Call.

"It's only fair," Jasper went on. "Consider it payback for making the right decision on the battlefield. And for all the lives you saved. Now we're even."

Call raised his eyebrows. Being picked last was always annoying, but this hardly seemed like a sufficient reward for lifesaving.

"I know," said Jasper. "I shouldn't have. Why am I so noble? I fight it but my better spirit always comes out ahead. You wouldn't understand."

"No one does," said Call. Aaron laughed.

It was Jasper's turn again, and in rapid succession he picked Gwenda, Tamara, and Kai, while Celia got two Gold Years named Malinda and Cindy.

"Well, this is going to suck," Gwenda said cheerfully once they were all grouped together. "Jasper, what were you thinking?"

"He was being noble," said Call.

"It's because he wants someone on his team who's going to make him look better," Tamara said.

Jasper flashed her a look of vast hurt, but he didn't contradict her.

"Teams," said Master Milagros, drawing all of their attention toward her. She was carrying a basket. "I'd like for each apprentice to take one of these metal rods and enchant it to be able to find another metal. The Magisterium is rich with metal deposits. You decide which metal you want to detect. The team that has found the most metal deposits in the next hour wins."

Looking over at Master Rufus, it seemed clear that their teacher was waiting for them to raise their hands and ask something, like, say, *how* to enchant the rods.

"Good luck!" Master Milagros said, and both teams rushed toward her to get their supplies.

Master Rufus shook his head and Call felt as though maybe he'd already failed some important test.

The metal was cool against Call's skin and heavier than he expected it to be. "Okay," he said to his team. "Now, uh, what do we do?"

Gwenda rolled her eyes and tucked a twist behind her ear. "See, Jasper."

Call's gratitude toward Gwenda for being willing to sit with him was swiftly evaporating.

"I was in *jail* and then *kidnapped*," Call snapped. "Not lying around on a beach drinking root beer floats."

"I heard it was Tamara who kidnapped you," Kai said, turning curious eyes in her direction.

"For the good of our team," Tamara said. "Just help us out."

"Fine," said Gwenda. "We're basically making these into dowsing rods for metal instead of water. Reach into the metal and think of the properties you want it to find. These rods have flecks of all other metals inside of them, so you can make them look for gold or copper or aluminum or whatever."

"Our best shot is to divide up the metals," said Tamara, which was really smart.

Gwenda nodded. "I'll take tungsten," she said. "Kai, you take copper. Tamara, you take gold, and —"

"*I* am the team captain," Jasper reminded them. "I will take gold. Tamara can have silver. The rest are fine. Call can have aluminum."

Call wasn't even sure what aluminum was except for the foil that his dad used to wrap up leftovers with. Still, there was nothing for him to do but agree. "Fine," he said, and started concentrating on the metal rod in his hand. He tried to think of it as a wand. After all, while in general being a mage hadn't been the way that TV shows portrayed it back in the regular world, those people often waved around wands and said *abracadabra*. He was going to wave around this one and it was going to lead him toward the most boring metal of all. Maybe he'd be able to wrap a lichen sandwich later.

Call concentrated, trying to find something that seemed

like the foil he grew up with inside what he was holding. He concentrated on silvery, shiny light until he felt a resonance.

You're doing it, Aaron encouraged.

Call felt movement in the metal rod in his hand. It rolled a little, then straightened, almost tugging him forward. He let it pull him, like Havoc dragging him on a leash. He could hear the voices of the others raised in excitement and dismay as they worked to find their own metals. Meanwhile, Call was being marched toward the lake. He wondered if the rod was going to drag him underwater. For all he knew there were aluminum deposits ten feet down. He shuddered a little and was relieved when the rod seemed to be maneuvering him around a large boulder.

He found himself squeezing along a narrow space between the boulder and the rock wall. Just when he was getting ridiculously claustrophobic, it opened out a little. He was in a space a little bigger than a telephone booth, the high cathedral ceiling visible overhead. Call glanced around. The rod had stopped twitching, but he didn't see anything that looked like aluminum.

Watch out, Aaron said suddenly, and Call stepped aside just as something whisked past his ear and hit the floor. He stared. It glimmered lightly — a ball of what was clearly aluminum. He eyed it for a long moment. "Did that just . . ."

"Callum Hunt."

It was a scratchy, half-hissing voice that Call knew well. He craned his head back and saw the fire lizard clinging to the rock above his head. Warren's jeweled scales glimmered in the light, and his red-gold eyes spun like pinwheels. "A gift for you."

Warren had dropped the aluminum? Call bent down and picked it up before straightening and eyeing the lizard suspiciously.

"Why are you helping me out?" Call asked.

Warren chuckled. "Old friends stick together, yes, old friends do." He cocked his head to the side. "I did not expect two of you."

I think he can sense me, Aaron thought, sounding a little nervous.

"Call!" Gwenda squeezed into the space beside him. Call nearly jumped out of his shoes. "What have you —" She broke off suddenly, staring up at Warren, her eyes widening. "Is that a fire elemental?"

"That's Warren," Call said. "He's just a lizard I know."

"Unkind," Warren hissed. "We are friends."

"And he talks," Gwenda marveled. "How'd you find him?"

"I think you mean how did he find *me*," said Call. "Warren shows up when he feels like it. What's up, Warren? You need a favor or something?"

"I come to warn you," Warren replied. "There has been much chatter in the elemental world. I have heard the water elementals in the river and the air elementals in the sky. A new great one has come."

"A new great what?" Gwenda blinked.

"The metal elementals speak of the cries of Automotones," said Warren.

"But Automotones is dead, or in chaos or whatever," said Call. "Come on, Warren. You're not making any sense."

Warren made a frustrated hissing sound. "The end is closer than you think."

Gwenda almost dropped her metal rod. "That sounds creepy!"

"Nah," said Call. "He always says that."

"Call!" It was Tamara, sounding worried. "Call, where are you?"

"So many friends." Warren's tongue shot out and licked his own eye, which was a habit he had that Call personally felt he should practice in private.

Tamara emerged from the crawl space, blinking at Gwenda and then at Warren. "Hey. I thought I heard you talking to someone and . . ." Her voice trailed off, probably because she realized how unflattering it was that Call talking to someone on his own was unusual enough to be a concern — although probably, sadly, accurate. "What's going on?"

"Nothing much," Call said at the same time Gwenda said, "Your creepy lizard friend was giving us a creepy lizard warning."

Tamara folded her arms and gave Call a stern look.

"He did say something about Automotones crying out or something," he admitted. "But I told him he had to be wrong, because Automotones is in chaos. Aaron sent him there when we were looking for my dad."

I sure did. Aaron sounded pleased.

Call turned to gesture toward Warren, but the little elemental was gone. Call threw up his hands in frustration. "Oh, come on! Warren? Get back here!"

"So this is how it happens with you guys?" Gwenda demanded. "Some weird lizard shows up and all of a sudden everything goes sideways and you're fighting a massive elemental or some Chaos-ridden army or whatever? Well, let me tell you, I am not in for any of that."

"No one's asking for your help," Call said grumpily, picking up his ball of aluminum.

That is kind of how it happens, though, Aaron said.

Just then there was a ringing noise, like a distant bell, followed by Master Milagros's voice, calling them back. They'd barely gotten to do any poking around. Call couldn't believe the exercise was already over.

"Did either of you find anything?" he asked.

Tamara shook her head. "I don't think there's any silver in these tunnels."

Gwenda looked a little smug. "I found a vein of tungsten back in the other room and marked it down. I ran into you when I started looking for a second one."

They squeezed through the tunnel to find Kai and Jasper excitedly marking their finds on a map. Call noticed that he was the only one who had an actual sample of the metal, though. He hoped that was a good thing, but when he showed Master Rufus, he looked over the aluminum ball in a puzzled manner.

Both Malinda and Cindy had found impressive amounts of their metals embedded in the walls. Celia's team had obviously won, although neither of the Masters made a big deal about it.

"Now that you've found so much metal in the Magisterium, tomorrow we will go to the library and discover the properties of each," Master Milagros announced. "What kinds of magic do each of the metals lend themselves to? And how would you fashion a weapon from what you've found today? We want to see your designs and ideas."

Celia, clearly expecting a prize instead of another assignment, gave a heavy sigh.

Master Milagros continued. "There's something else we are going to do today, something done very seldom, but which is not without precedent. Master Rufus and I have been discussing what would be most helpful to your learning and it's been decided that Gwenda and Jasper will become Master Rufus's apprentices and I will take on some of the orphaned apprentices from Masters who were lost in the recent battle. Right now, everyone is a little overloaded, and this is a way to help."

More Jasper? Why does the universe hate me? Call thought.

Tamara folded her arms over her chest. Call wasn't sure what it meant, but at least she wasn't jumping up and down for joy.

Celia, however, appeared to be fuming. She must be upset enough at having her boyfriend moved to another apprentice group, no less one with the Enemy of Death in it. This wasn't going to make things better between her and Call.

"Jasper hasn't made it much of a secret that he wanted to be Master Rufus's apprentice from the beginning," Gwenda said. "But why me?"

"Don't you remember?" Master Milagros said. "You asked to be reassigned."

For a moment, Gwenda looked as though she was going to choke, and Call abruptly recalled how she had come to their rooms a long time back to complain about Jasper and Celia making out. How she'd asked if they could persuade Master Rufus to take her on as an apprentice. Apparently, they weren't the only ones she'd discussed it with.

"But that was Bronze Year! And I definitely didn't want to move in *with Jasper*," Gwenda said, which so perfectly summed up Call's feelings that he couldn't help thinking it might be fun to have her as a roommate after all.

But no matter how much he liked them, having new apprentices in his group was going to be weird. It had always been him and Tamara and Aaron — and even if Tamara didn't know it, it still was. Besides, he had important stuff to work out with Tamara. How was he going to win her back with Jasper around all the time? How were they going to find time to talk?

How are you going to figure out a way to tell her about me? Aaron asked, and there was something in that thought that made Call remember how, to Aaron, this might feel like being replaced.

"Jasper and Gwenda, you're going to move into Tamara and Call's room, so pack up your things and we will reenchant your wristbands," said Master Rufus. "Tonight, I will meet with you privately to determine your strengths and weaknesses."

Jasper nodded, looking shocked. He'd spent his Iron Year trying to get into Master Rufus's apprentice group. Master Rufus was the most famous of the mage teachers and had an eye for picking apprentices who would go on to do important things — for good or for ill. He'd taught Constantine Madden, but he'd also taught prominent members of the Assembly and mages at the Collegium. Now, Jasper was finally getting his chance. Call wondered if it was still something he wanted.

"Okay," Jasper said slowly, as though he was still trying to process what was happening. Gwenda towed him away to pack. Celia went over to Master Milagros, probably to complain. Call decided he better go back to the room and make sure Havoc was on his best behavior for the move.

Tamara fell into step with him. "So," she said, "what do you think of Warren's warning?" With everything going on then, it was the last thing that Call expected her to say, but Tamara was a person who seldom let herself be distracted from what was important.

"Could Automotones have really escaped the void?" Call asked, although he didn't really expect an answer.

No, said Aaron. *Not possible.*

"I don't know," Tamara said. "But we could go to the library tonight to research. Maybe there was another elemental like Automotones."

"Like his cousin?" Call asked. "And you think that maybe Warren's friends mistook them because Automotones is the famous one?"

Tamara gave him an annoyed look. "Sure," she said. "Automotones is in all the elemental celebrity magazines."

Aaron chortled. *That was pretty good.*

Oh, shut up, Call thought, homing in on something he realized had almost passed him by. "We're going to the library tonight?" *Is this like a date? A study date?*

Tamara nodded. "I think we better check this out, just to be sure. Warren's annoying, but he's been right before." She put her hand to her chin. "We're going to need help, going through all those books. Jasper might do it. He's our new roommate now, after all."

So, not a date, then, Call realized. Aaron sang "I've Got a Lovely Bunch of Coconuts" in his head all the way through the corridors of the cave, just to cheer him up.

CHAPTER FIVE

THE MOVE DIDN'T take too long, Gwenda did
like dogs, and to both Tamara and Call's surprise, Jasper
and Gwenda agreed to accompany them to the library that
night before they went to meet with Master Rufus. Gwenda
seemed curious, and Jasper — well, Call wasn't sure why Jasper
did anything. Jasper watched Celia stride off to the Gallery
with half the other Gold Year students with a forlorn look on
his face, then squared his shoulders and followed Call and
Tamara to the library.

The library was one of Call's favorite places in the
Magisterium, not because he was particularly bookish but
because he'd spent a lot of good times there with Tamara and
Aaron. Now he, Tamara, Gwenda, and Jasper trooped in
under the inscription that read KNOWLEDGE IS FREE AND

SUBJECT TO NO RULE, and sat down at one of the long wooden tables in the center of the room.

"Okay," Tamara said, taking charge. "Here's what we're looking for. Stuff about Automotones — are there other elementals like him? And chaos — has anything ever come back from chaos? Do we know anything about the chaos realm?"

"Don't *you*?" Gwenda said, eyeing Call. "I mean, you're the chaos mage."

He shook his head. "No. No idea. I can send things through to chaos, but I don't have any idea what's on the other side."

They all split up and took different sections of the library; Call ended up in the chaos magic section, where there were a lot of books he guiltily realized he should probably have read already — books on the history of chaos mages, the meaning of counterweights, and the discovery of chaos magic. He was reaching for a book called *Soul and Void: Preliminary Theory* when Aaron spoke.

I need a body, he said. *I can't stay in your head forever.*

Call slumped against the bookshelves. He'd known this was coming, and it would be a relief to be alone in his own head, but it still felt a little rejecting. Plus, he had no idea how to accomplish it. "It's not that easy to just get a body," he murmured.

Maybe someone dead?

"We can't use a corpse — that's what happened to you last time. You got weird in there because the brain had been dead. And that was pushing your soul back into *you*. Imagine how it would be with some random other dead body." He paused. "And not a baby. That's what happened with me. You'd lose all your memories. You'd be a different person. A really little, helpless person."

I don't want to be a baby. Aaron sounded appalled. *And I definitely don't want to push out the soul of a baby.*

"We could go to the hospital," Call said, realizing how morbid the whole conversation was. "Find someone who's about to die?"

Wouldn't I just jump into their body and then die?

"We could fix them with magic?" Call suggested, though he knew this was unrealistic. Neither of them knew that much about healing magic.

Then we should probably patch them up and let them live, Aaron said with the annoying nobility that told Call that this Aaron was okay. He was alive now and not a scary undead monster and there was a big part of Call that wanted to quit while they were ahead, even if it meant Aaron lived in his skull forever.

"If you keep shooting down all my suggestions, you're going to be stuck here," Call reminded him.

From behind a nearby bookcase, he heard someone giggling. He peered around, worrying that someone had heard him talking to himself. Instead, he saw Tamara sitting on the table, swinging her legs, with Jasper beside her, apparently saying something amusing. Call narrowed his eyes.

We'll think of something. Aaron sounded desperate.

We could kill someone, thought Call, eyes narrowing further as he watched Tamara giggle again and Jasper preen. He was definitely flirting. *We could kill Jasper, for instance.*

We're not going to kill Jasper. I don't want to be a murderer.

You killed Master Joseph, Call thought, and then was surprised at himself. He wouldn't have said that to Aaron out loud. He hadn't wanted to mention anything that had happened during that horrible time. But he couldn't seem to stop thinking. *You practically pulled off his head like a tomato —*

I wasn't myself, Aaron protested. Call didn't say anything. He heard Tamara giggle again but didn't have the heart to look — he didn't have any claim on her. She could go out with Jasper if she wanted, even if the thought made Call want to smash his own head against a stalactite.

There was no point being angry at Aaron either. None of this was Aaron's fault. It was Master Joseph's fault. Alex Strike's fault. Constantine Madden's fault. And Call's own fault.

I guess jumping from one body to another is always going to be murder, Aaron thought somberly. *You're always killing someone else's soul. That's why it's evil. That's why all that Enemy of Death stuff was wrong. It turned out to cause a lot of death instead of reversing it.*

I guess so. Call carried *Soul and Void: Preliminary Theory* over to the table, where Gwenda had already joined Tamara and Jasper. They were chattering about Automotones, Tamara and Jasper telling Gwenda about the battle at Alastair's old car lot, especially Havoc's heroics.

Do you remember? Call thought, but Aaron had gone silent in his mind.

It wasn't fair. He felt bad about hurting Aaron's feelings, but it was impossible not to think stupid, awful stuff. Horrible things floated to the surface of his mind all the time and he couldn't stop them from coming. In the past, he'd barely restrained himself from saying the worst of his thoughts out loud; how was he supposed to restrain himself from thinking them? And then Aaron got to go off to hide in the back of his head and not reveal anything. Maybe Aaron's thoughts were even worse than Call's, but Call would never know.

From the table laden with books, he heard Gwenda speak. "So Call dragged you to this enormous car graveyard looking for his father and then an elemental attacked you, and Call *still* didn't tell you that he was the Enemy of Death?"

"I think it was hard to say out loud," Jasper said, surprising Call. "He probably wasn't even sure we'd believe him. I wouldn't have. Of course I would have pretended to at the time, because I was kidnapped and you should never tell your kidnapper that he's a crazy person."

"You get kidnapped a lot," Gwenda said, gloriously unsympathetic.

"I do, now that you mention it," said Jasper. "Why am I defending Call again? He's the *reason* I am always getting kidnapped."

"Because you're super good friends?" Gwenda said, sounding confused. "You're his sidekick. Well, one of his sidekicks."

"That's true," said Tamara. "Havoc is really his main sidckick."

"No, no, no, no, no!" Jasper said, clearly appalled. "You can't really have thought of me that way. I am his rival! Call and I are always going head to head, toe to toe, in contests of war and love. And I win as often as I lose! I am his rival!"

"If you say so," Gwenda said.

Call, despite everything else, had to smile.

Gwenda checked her watch. "We have to go meet with Master Rufus," she said, sounding relieved. "Which is fine, because this is kind of boring. I can't believe we're here because a lizard dropped a hint."

"Warren's been right before," said Call, not sure if he was defending Warren or himself. "We'll take these books back to the rooms and keep going through them until we find something."

"Whatever floats your boat," said Gwenda. She made a clicking noise at Jasper, who looked incredulous. "Come on. Time's a-wasting."

"People click at *dogs*," Jasper protested, following Gwenda from the room. "You can't click at me."

"Click," Gwenda said cheerfully. "Click, click."

Jasper's protests were muffled as he and Gwenda moved out of earshot. Shaking her head, Tamara divided up the book burden between herself and Call. "Maybe we are being paranoid," she said as they left the library. "Maybe Warren really didn't mean anything."

"You can hardly blame us for being paranoid after everything we've been through," said Call. He was wishing Aaron would come into his head again and tell him the right thing to say to Tamara, who looked tired and worried, but Aaron remained stubbornly absent.

Tamara ducked her head. "I guess not."

What was she *thinking*? Call wanted to bang his head on a wall, but they'd reached their rooms and Tamara was letting them in with her wristband. They dumped their books on the table. Call was about to suggest they head to the Gallery for a snack when Tamara picked up *Soul and Void* and glanced at the back.

"'The opposite of chaos,'" she read, in a low voice, "'is the human soul.'" She swallowed hard. "Call, I — I'm sorry. Not that I told you not to bring back Aaron — but that I didn't try harder to understand why you felt like you needed to. Everyone was telling you that you were responsible for his death. Everyone was treating you like it was your fault. You must have felt like the only way to fix things was to bring him back."

Call knew it was probably a bad idea to be honest. But he didn't know what else to do, or what else to say. "I didn't want Aaron back so I'd feel better," he said. "I mean, yeah, I felt guilty. But I was scared to do it, too. I'm always scared of what might happen if I'm not always watching myself, checking to make sure I don't go full evil. But Aaron was my friend, and he had faith in me, and I didn't want him to be dead. That was all."

Tamara's eyes shone, as though she was holding back the edge of tears. "And I went off and left you," she said. "You must have thought I had no faith in you at all. I knew I was wrong the minute I got back to the Magisterium. I'd been thinking that the mages would save us all, the Assembly would help, that they were grown-ups and we were kids, but they're just flawed people. They can't fix everything."

"No one can fix everything," said Call. Tamara looked so sad, he wanted desperately to hug her, but would she want that? "It's not your fault you trusted them —"

"I trust *you*," she said. "You're my friend, Call, and I —"

"I don't want to just be your friend," he said.

She looked at him wide-eyed, like she couldn't believe he said that. Call could feel his heart pounding through his whole body. He wasn't sure he believed he'd said it either. "I'm sorry," he said. "But it's the truth. I like you, Tamara. In fact, I —"

She rose up on her tiptoes and kissed him. It felt like lightning had zapped Call's whole body. The first time they'd ever kissed, he'd been too stunned to really respond, but this time he wrapped his arms around her just like he'd wanted to before. And Tamara put her arms around *him*, and that was amazing, and she stroked his cheek gently while he kissed her, and that was even more amazing. She smelled like rosewater, and he was pretty sure this was the best kiss anyone in history had ever had and would definitely have gotten an Olympic ten in kissing if the Olympics graded this kind of thing.

AUGH! I AM STILL IN HERE! came the shout in Call's

head, causing Call to pull away from Tamara. It was Aaron, apparently horrified out of his sulk by all the kissing.

"Call?" Tamara asked, confused. She was looking at him with a kind of dreamy half smile on her face that made him just want to kiss her again, but she'd probably be really angry when she found out about Aaron.

"Uh," said Call, casting about for something, some reason to stop that would mean they could start up again later. "I think we're moving too fast. I think we need to . . ." There, Call's thoughts deserted him.

STOP, Aaron said.

"Stop," Call echoed.

Tamara blinked at him, looking hurt. "Okay," she said in a small voice. "But I thought this was what you wanted."

"Oh, I do!" Call said, maybe a little bit too eagerly. "I really, really do. It's only . . ."

That I think we should, um, take a break to make sure you're sure, Aaron said.

Call repeated the words. They sounded good. Thoughtful. Mature. Tamara was looking at him weirdly again, though.

We want to make sure we are building on a foundation of trust, Aaron said.

Call said that, too, trying to invest the words with conviction, trying to be the person who believed them. Tamara folded her arms across her chest and looked at him with narrowed eyes.

"You sound like Aaron," she told him.

"That's a good thing, right?" Call asked.

"It's something," she said, which did not sound entirely like agreement. "I guess we both miss him in our own way." She put her hand on his cheek, warm against his skin. "Good night, Call."

And with that, she went off to her room, leaving Call to go to his own and throw himself onto the little bed. Havoc jumped up, circling around before sitting directly on Call's feet, but Call couldn't even summon up the energy to care.

Things had been going so well with Tamara that he'd almost forgotten that he had another secret. She'd already put up with so much. And would she even believe him?

Call, Aaron said. *We have to talk about something.*

I know what you're going to say, Call told him, looking up at the shimmering mica ceiling above him, remembering how great it had been for that one moment when they were together and everything else hadn't mattered. *That I should just trust her. And I know I should. I should tell her. But I just want things to be normal.*

That's not it. I found something in your head. Something — weird.

Something in his *head*? Call closed his eyes. A huge weariness had come over him. Whatever it was Aaron knew, he didn't want to hear about it. *Not now,* he said. *Just not now.*

CHAPTER SIX

CALL DREAMED, AND in his dream, he was a grown-up mage in a city he didn't recognize. He lifted his hands and black lightning — chaos lightning — sparked between them. He felt a sense of surety and overwhelming power. It reminded him of the feeling he'd had when chaos was coursing through his body, except now he knew how to channel it.

This must have been what it felt like to be Constantine Madden.

The black fire shot from his fingers. It was as if he were Zeus; he could burn the whole world and it would be easy. With movements of his fingers, he guided the destructive fire, striking down other mages as they tried to run. Fire burst from the roofs of buildings. A stone clock tower was burning. He had no counterweight, but it didn't matter. Nothing mattered. Nothing mattered but power.

↑ ≈ △ ○ @

Call sat up, gasping. His hair was plastered to his forehead with sweat. It took him several long moments to remember who he was and where he was — in his own bed in the Magisterium.

He kicked the covers away, hoping the shock of cold air would wake him up and push him further from the dream. It had been horrible, in a wonderful sort of way . . .

Are you all right? Aaron sounded worried.

I think so, Call said. *I mean, yeah. It was a nightmare, is all.*

It was Constantine, Aaron said. *His memories. It had to have been.*

I've had weird dreams before, Call said. *They don't necessarily mean anything.*

I'm sorry about before, Aaron said. *Let me tell you what I found, okay? Then we can maybe figure out how to handle . . . kissing . . . while I'm still here.*

Call sighed. "Probably by just not doing it," he said glumly. At least in his bedroom he could talk out loud to Aaron without anyone thinking he'd lost his mind. "Okay, shoot."

There's something locked up in your head, Aaron said. *I don't know how to describe it, but being in here is like being in a big space with windows. I can look out of them and I'm looking out of your eyes. There are currents, emotions, that move past me, and your thoughts are like words in my mind. But when we weren't talking, before, it was like I bumped up against a locked door. In the middle of the room. There's something closed away inside it.*

"Like a repressed memory?" Call said, puzzled.

I think it's Constantine's memories, said Aaron. *I think someone shut them away in here so you wouldn't have access to them.*

"Why would anyone do that?"

I don't know. Aaron sounded frustrated. *Maybe when he jumped into your body, because you were a baby, your mind couldn't handle all of the memories, so they got shut away.*

It made a kind of sense. "Or maybe they would have made me realize I was an adult, trapped in a baby's body. Maybe he thought that would make him go insane?"

I don't know, but I think we should open them.

Call was up and out of the bed, shaking his head, though he knew Aaron couldn't see him. "No. No!"

Why not?

"The whole time I was with Master Joseph, every time I was around Anastasia Tarquin, all they wanted was for me to remember being Constantine Madden, because they thought those memories would, I don't know, *overwrite* my own. What if the memories make me stop being Call?"

Aaron was quiet for a long moment. *I guess I figured they would just be memories and it would be like the way I am in your head. I'm still me, even if I hear your thoughts.*

"But Constantine's soul was *my* soul. Maybe they will feel like my memories. But even if they don't, what if they're really, really bad?" He was afraid, he realized, of more than just the possibility of turning into Constantine. He was afraid of facing all the terrible things that Constantine had really done. What if Call remembered every ugly, awful thing? What if he had to remember the death of his own mother?

I guess I didn't think about any of that, Aaron said. *But if you ever want to look at the memories, I'm here in your head, too. I will do everything I can to make sure that you stay you, okay?*

Call felt like a coward. "Let me think about it."

It was early, but he knew he wasn't going to be able to get back to sleep. Instead, he got up, got his towel and his change of clothes, and headed to the bathing room, Havoc padding along behind him. He washed up quickly while Havoc popped soap bubbles with his tongue, sneezing and then growling at the bubbles.

After the bath, Call headed back into his room and was startled by Jasper, shirtless, doing stretches in the common area.

"What are you doing?" Call demanded.

"Limbering up for the day ahead," Jasper said, as though Call were the weird one. "Getting into the right mental place for magic."

"Ah," Call said. "Sure."

By the time he got back from walking Havoc, both of the girls were up, Gwenda with a purple silk cap over her twists, Tamara yawning as she took her toothpaste into the bathing area. The reality that Jasper and Gwenda were really Call's new roommates and in his apprentice group was sinking in and he still wasn't sure how he felt about it. On the plus side, at least they hadn't walked in on him and Tamara kissing.

Call had just put down some kibble for Havoc when the door opened and Master Rufus came in. "Today, apprentices, we're going to continue to learn about metal, from both a scientific and magical perspective. Call, you will be joining us after you meet with a member of the Assembly."

"That doesn't sound good," Call said.

"This is an informal meeting and Mr. Rajavi has assured me that very little time will be taken away from your classes." Master Rufus didn't seem particularly concerned, which was reassuring. And Call knew Mr. Rajavi. Maybe it wouldn't be so bad.

"My dad's here?" Tamara asked.

"He wanted me to give you his regards," said Master Rufus. "He was sorry he couldn't see you, but there are rules against apprentices getting visitors."

Unless that apprentice was a Makar who might also be an Evil Overlord. Then you got a lot of visitors.

"Call, Mr. Rajavi will be waiting for you in my office. I will accompany the rest of you to the Refectory." And with that, they were off, leaving Call to eat some cereal and go to Master Rufus's office alone.

Call took the path that led alongside one of the Magisterium's many underground rivers. It glowed eerie blue in the light of the moss. On the way, he peered around, looking for Warren. He even called the little lizard's name a few times, his voice echoing through the caverns. He was sure he'd see Warren during the short boat trip, but by the time he got to the far bank, he decided Warren was avoiding him.

When Call reached Rufus's door, he tapped on it and heard Mr. Rajavi's voice echo from inside: "Come in." The office looked much as it always had. The same papers were tacked to the walls, covered in what Call now recognized as alchemical equations. The big couch was gone, replaced by more bookshelves, and the old workstation had been replaced by one made of a gleaming clear material — quartz, Call guessed. Tamara's father sat behind Rufus's rolltop desk.

Oh, God, Call thought. *Tamara's father.* And he'd just kissed Tamara. Was that why Mr. Rajavi was here?

Don't be totally ridiculous, said Aaron. *Do you think he's psychic or something?*

Kimiya was grounded for making out with Evil Overlord Alex — Tamara had said so. Mr. Rajavi had a well-established policy of not liking his children making out with Evil Overlords.

Call slid into the chair opposite the desk, eyes wide. Mr. Rajavi gazed at him with an unsmiling expression. He wore an expensive-looking black suit and a thick gold watch on one wrist. His beard was perfectly trimmed.

I need to say something about Tamara, Call thought.

You really don't, said Aaron, sounding alarmed.

I have to reassure him, Call protested.

Reassure him about what? You DID kiss Tamara. Just keep your mouth shut, Call.

"My intentions are honorable!" Call blurted. He wanted to say more, but Aaron had set up a loud angry buzzing in his head, like a giant bee.

Mr. Rajavi blinked. "That's good, son. It's good to hear that despite having the soul of Constantine Madden, you want to live an honorable life."

Narrow escape, Aaron muttered. At least he'd stopped the bee noise. Call shifted uncomfortably in his chair.

"I'll cut to the chase," Tamara's father said. "Your mother, Anastasia Tarquin, has been asking for you."

"She's not my mother." A wave of anger passed over Call, erasing his previous embarrassment. "She was Constantine Madden's mother, and I am *not him*."

Mr. Rajavi smiled thinly. "I like your conviction. And I know my daughter thinks highly of you. Then again, I've started to be suspicious of those my daughters think highly of."

Maybe you should *tell him you kissed Tamara*, said Aaron. *He's a jerk.*

He was always like this, Call said. *You just never saw it because he wasn't like that to you.*

Call felt instantly bad for having thought that, but he didn't want to let the silence stretch out too long while he tried to explain stuff to Aaron. "If you mean Alex Strike, I'm glad he's dead, too," Call said bluntly. "But I don't want to see Anastasia."

"She's in the Panopticon," said Mr. Rajavi. "Her sentencing was this afternoon. She's been condemned to death."

That shook Call. He tried not to show it, but his hands tightened on the arms of his chair. Maybe he should agree to see her, but trying to imagine himself back in the Panopticon, on the other side of the magical glass, was awful. Besides, he didn't have anything to say to Anastasia. He couldn't help her. And he didn't want to keep pretending to be okay with her calling him Constantine.

He thought about the memories Aaron had found locked away in his head. Maybe if he looked at those, he would have some of the feelings for her that she hoped he would. But that only made him more determined not to unlock those memories.

"Do I have to go?" Call asked.

"Of course not," Mr. Rajavi said. He seemed relieved at the thought that Call was really saying no. Maybe he didn't want to go to the Panopticon either. "If you change your mind, tell Master Rufus."

Call stood up, assuming the meeting was over, only to have Mr. Rajavi stay where he was. After an awkward moment, Call sat down again. "Is there something else?"

"An offer. You're graduating from the Magisterium soon. Once you finish your Gold Year, you will be a mage in earnest and a very powerful one, a Makar. I want you to go to the

Collegium. I will make sure you get accepted into the best programs there. I will clear a path for you to be a very important mage, perhaps an Assembly member yourself one day. But we want you to stop using chaos magic, except with the explicit permission of the Assembly. We want you to be *our* Makar."

Call was astonished. It wasn't like he was running around using chaos magic all the time, for fun. But this was the same Mr. Rajavi who'd gotten Aaron to perform tricks with chaos magic at one of his parties. How had that been okay, but this wasn't?

Maybe the Assembly would give you permission to do chaos tricks at parties, too, Aaron said with surprising cynicism.

"How would you know?" Call asked.

Mr. Rajavi's eyebrows went up. Call supposed it didn't sound like the question of someone who was planning on being honest.

"Well," Mr. Rajavi said. "We would choose a new counterweight for you."

A new counterweight? Call was surprised at the depths of his revulsion at the thought. Aaron was his best friend. That was why he'd been willing to be Aaron's counterweight and why Aaron had been his.

I'm still your best friend, Aaron said. *If you start thinking like I am dead, it's really going to freak me out.*

"What if I don't agree?" Call asked Mr. Rajavi.

"Let's just hope that you do," he said, a promise and a threat all in one.

"I've got to think about it," Call replied.

Mr. Rajavi stood and extended his hand to Call, who got up to shake it. Call realized again how much taller he'd grown. He was looking down at Mr. Rajavi's head.

"Think well," Mr. Rajavi said. "You've got a bright future ahead of you."

On Call's stiff-legged walk back through the tunnels, he considered Anastasia and the Assembly's offer. He thought about Alastair, too, and his promise that once Gold Year was over they could travel and establish themselves in a new place with new identities.

Call came to where the rest of his apprentice group was training. Tamara was shaping her metal into a shining circle, liquid and dazzling. Jasper was poking some gold nuggets, while Gwenda was attempting to coax a mushy puddle of bronze into a bracelet. Master Rufus was sitting on a rock, looking to be a bit in despair.

If Call went away with Alastair, he would never see any of them again, but if he accepted the Assembly's offer, he could see them whenever he wanted. They could all go to the Collegium together. He wouldn't do any more chaos magic; it wasn't like he wanted to do it anyway. Mr. Rajavi might not even ground Tamara for dating him.

You're forgetting about one thing, Aaron said.

What's that? Call asked.

Me.

CHAPTER SEVEN

A T L U N C H I N the Refectory, Gwenda and Tamara chatted animatedly. Jasper seemed sunk in gloom, gazing frequently over at the nearby table where Celia sat, surrounded by her other Gold and Silver Year friends. Call recognized some of them — a quiet boy with brown hair named Charlie, and a girl with a short black pixie cut whose name, he thought, was Jessie. But quite a few were total strangers to him. Maybe because he'd spent so much time away from the Magisterium, he realized — and maybe because even when he'd been there he'd been too wrapped up in his comfortable group of three to notice much.

Sometimes Jasper would wave at Celia. She would wave back graciously, ignoring everyone else at the table. Tamara just rolled her eyes — they were all laughing and joking around, except Call, who stayed quiet. He could sense Aaron's tension. Aaron had always loved these kinds of big groups, flourishing on all the humor and affection.

It's like being a ghost, Aaron said now. *I can see everything, but I can't do anything. Or say anything.*

"What is going on with you, Jasper?" Gwenda said finally, after he'd exchanged another weird wave with Celia. "Are you guys together or not?"

"It's complicated," said Jasper. "Celia wants me to renounce Call and lodge a protest about being put into Master Rufus's apprentice group."

"That's ridiculous," said Kai. "Half the school would kill to be Rufus's student."

"Well, he does seem to *LIKE KILLERS*," called Celia, who had clearly overheard and was glaring.

They all dropped their voices. "Well, you obviously can't do that," whispered Gwenda.

"No, of course not," said Jasper.

"Call's your friend," said Rafe.

"It's not that," Jasper protested. "It's about not giving in! A deWinter doesn't do what he's told! A deWinter is independent!"

Call thought about how Jasper's father wasn't independent at all. He was locked away in the Panopticon, besmirching the deWinter name. Jasper liked to complain — a *lot* — about little stuff, but never about his dad's situation. It must weigh on him, though.

"Celia can't keep being so ridiculous," said Tamara. "It's unbelievable she's getting any support."

"I'd say about half the school feels like she does," said Kai in a low voice. "There are a lot of people who don't like or trust Call, and some of them think he's basically just the Enemy of Death in a Gold Year uniform."

"What about the people who actually like me?" said Call, feeling sick.

"They're all at this table," said Gwenda.

"That's not true!" Tamara protested. "There are people who like you, Call. And Havoc likes you. And Warren."

"Warren doesn't like anyone," said Call, pushing his plate away. He thought about his dream of the Collegium — wouldn't it just be more of this?

Kai suddenly stood up. His brown eyes met Call's and he shook his head sadly. "I'm sorry," he said, and crossed the room to sit down at Celia's table.

They all stared after him, stunned. Rafe broke the silence. "Charlie's his boyfriend, and he's completely on Celia's side," he said. "You have to understand — it's been really hard on Kai."

Jasper looked grim. "Battle lines are being drawn," he said, and for once, he wasn't kidding around. Call almost imagined he could see a thin glowing line separating their table from Celia's.

Dragging a fork through his lichen, Call knew that he was going to have to do something. He just wished he knew what.

↑ ≈ △ ○ ℓ

After lunch, exercises were outside in the woods and included Gold Years and Iron Years. They were to accompany the younger kids as they explored the area around the Magisterium and tried out some newly learned magic.

"Don't let them wander off," Master Rufus said. "This will be good for all of you, to take responsibility for younger mages, to help them and also to realize how far you've come in your own studies."

"None of them are going to want to partner with me," Call said to Tamara, then was a little ashamed. His friends already had to deal with the hostility that people they cared about felt toward Call. He didn't have to complain on top of it.

Tamara patted him reassuringly on the shoulder. "Maybe there's a tiny evil one." He glowered at her and she smiled cheerfully back at him. "That's the spirit. Your evil little fan will like that."

He laughed despite himself.

Meanwhile, Jasper was puffing himself up with the thought that someone was going to be impressed with him. "I have a lot of wisdom to pass on," he was saying to Gwenda. "The important thing is that I find an apprentice worthy of me."

"I really think none of them deserve you," Gwenda told him, and he nodded thoughtfully.

"You're so right."

"Oh," she said. "I know I am."

Once they were through the Mission Gate, Call couldn't help noticing that the woods were strangely quiet. No bird calls came from the trees. He couldn't even hear crickets.

He looked toward the others. Tamara and Master Rufus had paused, too. The silence was truly eerie. Woods were never really quiet — there was always birdsong, or the sound of distant animals in the underbrush. But there was nothing. Call was about to say something to Master Rufus when the Magisterium gates opened again, and more and more apprentices filed out with their Masters. Suddenly it was harder to hear the silence of the woods over the human chatter.

"We've already paired you up," Master Rockmaple said, loudly enough that the apprentices began to quiet down. "I will call out the name of a Gold Year and then the Iron Year they are to be paired with."

A breeze blew through the trees, and in the moment after Master Rockmaple finished speaking Call was unnerved again to hear the whistle of wind through branches and nothing more. No animal sounds. But there was the sound of something else. It sounded to Call like something familiar.

"Rockmaple," Master Rufus said, "I think we should go back inside and postpone this exercise for another —"

Then Call remembered. It was the sound he had heard when he and his father had gone to Niagara Falls once. An enormously loud rushing noise, as if the air were splintering.

A buzz rose among the apprentices, but there was no time to do anything. Before Master Rufus could even finish his sentence, high over the trees an elemental appeared.

Call heard Tamara gasp. "A *dragon*."

The dragon was massive, shiny black and sinuous, with small, membranous wings and enormous, fang-lined jaws. Its eyes were a brilliant red. A human rider sat on its back — one in a long cloak that was whipped by the wind.

Call reached for Tamara; she grabbed his hand and held it. He could *feel* Aaron inside his head, flinching in disbelief — and horror.

Impossibly, the rider was Alex. Changed, but still recognizable, even though a nimbus of darkness surrounded his head. It was as if someone had cut the light out of the sky surrounding him. His eyes were enormous black holes that shimmered, as though full of stars.

Apprentices screamed. People started running back toward the Magisterium. Not all of them recognized Alex, but they definitely recognized bad news when they saw it. Call and Tamara stood their ground, though Master Rufus had moved to block them from Alex's direct view.

He's dead. Aaron sounded stunned. *He's got to be dead. He was sucked into chaos.*

The dragon opened its enormous jaws and out came black fire. It seared across the tops of the surrounding trees, setting them aflame. They burned without light, without heat. Call remembered his dream, the black flame spreading from his hands. The dragon was breathing pure chaos fire.

"Quickly, everyone inside!" Master Rufus shouted. He gestured for the students to get back. "Tamara! Call! Get out of here!" The Masters were running, circling the students in order to herd them back to the Magisterium gates. Iron Years were running, almost tripping over one another in their eagerness to get back toward the gates.

"Wait!" shouted one of the Masters. "Stay close —"

But it was too late. The dragon swooped down, Alex clinging to its back, and caught two Iron Years. One of them was Axel, the little kid who'd been curious about Call when he'd first arrived at the Magisterium. He looked terrified, but he wasn't crying. He looked like he was trying to bite the chaos dragon's claws. Next to him was an Iron Year girl screaming as she tried to kick her way free. But the dragon held fast, swooping up into the sky with the Iron Years gripped tightly in its claws.

Astride the dragon, grinning now, Alex shouted, his voice booming across the forest. "Stop! All Masters of the Magisterium, stop where you are! I am Alexander Strike, the first ever Devoured of chaos, and I will destroy you all unless you follow my commands."

A Devoured of chaos? Call looked over at Master Rufus, but Master Rufus was intent on staring at Alex. He looked enraged. All the Masters did, but they had stopped in their tracks, knowing they had no choice. Above them, they could hear the Iron Years screaming, their cries carried thinly on the wind.

Call turned to Tamara. She was trembling with fury.

"We have to do something," she said. The black flames licked higher, eating up more of the woods. *Fire*, Call thought. He had put out fire before.

It nearly killed you, Aaron protested. *Now, without a counterweight —*

Alex was still talking. "First, release Anastasia Tarquin from captivity or I will drop these brats into the fire and then finish off the rest of you. *After* you watch them burn."

A murmur ran through the crowd. *Anastasia Tarquin?* Not everyone knew she had been Alex's stepmother; even Call was astonished Alex cared enough to bother springing her from prison.

It was Master Rufus who stepped forward to speak. "You must give us time," he called. "We have to contact the Panopticon."

Alex was grinning savagely. Call could only imagine the pleasure he was getting out of ordering around his old teachers. "Get a tornado phone out here in five minutes, or I'll toast a tot."

Master Rockmaple turned and plunged into the Magisterium.

"Call and Tamara," Alex said, turning his star-blackened gaze to them. His face looked like parchment behind which brilliant black light was burning. "What a great reunion!" He threw his head back and laughed.

"You should have stayed in the void," Call shouted as he concentrated on pulling the air away from the chaos fire eating away at the trees. But no matter how he pulled, the flames didn't so much as flicker. They weren't like regular fire, fed on air. Call wasn't sure what they fed on, but as his magic flowed toward them, he felt neither heat nor light. If the opposite of chaos was soul, then he feared the fire fed on the substance of the world itself.

He couldn't put out the fire that way, but he was a Makar. He should be able to control it. He sent his power toward the licking flames of chaos, concentrating on stopping its spread. It seemed like it was working — the fire began to ebb, burning itself out with nothing more to feed on.

"And you should have never been born," Alex told him, looking delighted to do so. "You are a parody of all that the Enemy of Death was, you flimsy imitation."

"He's a Devoured," Tamara said quietly to Call. "That's kind of like being an elemental. You could control a chaos elemental, right?"

Good idea, Aaron thought.

Call smiled with vengeful hope. If he could control Alex, he would be hard-pressed not to make him do something stupid and humiliating — after, of course, setting down the Iron Year kids. He reached out again, this time not toward the fire itself but toward Alex —

— only to hit what felt like a wall of sticky nothing. He felt his power being pulled toward Alex and yanked it back with what felt like physical force. Whatever Alex had become, he was too powerful for Call to control.

Master Rockmaple raced back through the Mission Gate with Master North and Mr. Rajavi — who had apparently not made it off the grounds of the Magisterium. Master North carried a tornado phone.

Tamara looked over at her father. He gave her a quick glance in return but didn't speak to her, which was probably the right move. Better for Alex not to be reminded of their relationship. Better for Alex not to think of a new way to hurt one of them.

"We can't really give in to this," Master North was saying. Then he spotted the kids hanging from the claws of the dragon, both of them looking increasingly panicked, increasingly sure they were going to be fed to chaos.

"For now," Mr. Rajavi said, activating the tornado phone.

On the other end was a guard at the Panopticon. Call recognized the uniform with a shudder.

"We need you to get Anastasia Tarquin and prepare her for release. But bring her here first. We need to see her and that she is all right as she is set free," Mr. Rajavi said.

"Anastasia *Tarquin*?" demanded the guard, stunned. "On whose authority?"

"On behalf of the Assembly, which I speak for," Mr. Rajavi said as the guard seemed to slowly realize both who he was talking to and the confusion of what was happening in the background. He paled and ran off.

Up on his dragon, Alex smiled, smug. The dragon opened its claws and the girl slipped, her scream carrying to them. The dragon caught her again, as though she were a ball and it was playing a game. Her screams went on and on.

"Stop!" cried Mr. Rajavi. "We're giving you what you want! Only return the children —"

"Sure, I'll send them back — lightly seared," said Alex, laughing. It occurred to Call that this was what Alex had always wanted to be. This was what he'd always thought the Enemy of Death was supposed to be like: this maniacal, howling horror.

"The children are innocent," said Master Rufus. "They have done nothing to you. Take me."

"Drew was innocent," snarled Alex. Call struggled not to point out that this wasn't in the least bit true. He didn't think it would be helpful. "You murdered him, all of you. You are the teachers of lies!"

"He's going to freak out," Tamara whispered, her face pale. "We have to do something —"

"She's here!" called Master North. Through the swirling air of the tornado phone, they could see Anastasia in the baggy uniform of a Panopticon prisoner, being led out the front door of the jail by two burly guards. She was blinking but clearly unharmed.

Alex made a growling noise. "Set her free!"

The guards stepped aside, and Anastasia looked around in stunned amazement. It was clear she had no idea what was going on. Her voice was audible, barely, through the phone. "What's happening? Who's there?"

"Let the children go!" called Rufus.

Alex smiled unpleasantly. "Hmmm. Should I really?"

"You'd better!" Tamara yelled. "Everyone knows what Anastasia looks like and everyone knows she's a traitor. If you don't get to her first, any passing mage might grab her and throw her back in prison, or worse!"

Alex bared his teeth. The whole crowd tensed — and the dragon reared forward and swooped, opening its claws. The two Iron Years tumbled free, hurtling toward the ground and then slowing just before they hit. They both sat up, to Call's relief. Axel was holding his arm, though, and Call supposed that the Masters hadn't been able to cushion him enough.

Master Rockmaple ran toward the children. Alex's dragon reared back, letting out a puff of black fire. "You will not follow me," Alex said, and thrust out his hand.

Darkness poured from it. Call remembered his dream again. A whole city torn apart by chaos.

The darkness began to form a whirling void, like a black, sucking funnel. As it spread toward the Magisterium, it sucked in leaves and stones. It seared the ground as it passed.

It was closest to Master Rockmaple, because he had run to grab the children. He raised his hands, and fire blazed between them. With a stern look, he hurled fire toward the chaos —

And the black wave surged forward and enveloped him. With a howl, he was dragged into the void.

He was gone.

People were screaming again, turning to run back into the Magisterium, but the press of bodies created a blockage at the gates. They were trapping themselves outside. It was going to be a massacre.

Call thrust his own hand out, reaching down inside himself. *The counterweight to chaos is the soul.* He knew the soul tap, how to find the energy of his own life-force, and he reached for it heedlessly, ignoring the almost physical pain as he drew on it.

Use me! Aaron called. *Use my energy, too!*

Call only shook his head. His hair whipped on the wind from the chaos void. Tamara was yanking on his arm, trying to get him to back away. He bent his fingers slightly, the way he had in his dream —

The void began to fragment, coming apart in pieces like black glass shattering.

But darkness was all around Call and he felt himself falling.

CHAPTER EIGHT

CALL WOKE WITH a start. For a moment, he thought that he was lost in chaos, until he heard the familiar hum of voices and the distinct mineral smell of the caves of the Magisterium. He sat up, startling Master Amaranth.

He was in the infirmary. Call relaxed and slumped back on the pillow.

The mage came over to him, her coppery hair pulled back and her snake coiled around her head like some enormous headband. Today, it was a bright yellow green that turned to blue and then purple as Call watched. A moment later, red stripes emerged on its scales.

You almost died, Aaron said in his head.

"Oh," Call said. He remembered something like that.

Something about the hole ripped into chaos and trying to close it and trying to tap into his own soul.

I tried to hold on to you, but it felt like you were slipping away, Aaron went on. He sounded panicked and angry. Call guessed that made sense. If he'd died, Aaron would have died, too.

That is NOT the point — Aaron began, but Master Amaranth interrupted.

"Against my advice, your friend is still here," she said.

Call thought for a bizarre moment that she meant Aaron, before he whirled around to see Tamara sitting on the cot beside him. She set down the anatomy book she'd been reading and hurried over to his bed.

"Sorry," he said, although whether he was saying it to her or to Aaron, he wasn't sure. "I guess I am not so good at defeating my enemies, huh?"

"Don't be an idiot," said Tamara fondly. "You don't have anything to be sorry for."

You don't understand, Aaron said. *I wasn't going to die. If your soul was used up, I would have been alone in here.*

Call guessed that was one way that Aaron could get a body.

That's not funny, said Aaron.

Tamara sat down in the chair next to his cot. She was smiling, and he was incredibly relieved to see her, too. Things hadn't been looking good when he lost consciousness. "You're all right?" he said. "Everyone's okay?"

"Mostly," Tamara said. "You tore Alex's chaos tornado apart, and then you passed out and I didn't *exactly* notice what else was going on." She blushed. "But basically Alex escaped in all the yelling." She bit her lip. "We lost Master Rockmaple, too."

"I'm sorry," Call said again. He knew he should have acted earlier.

"I told you it's not your fault," Tamara said, with a return of her usual bossiness. "I don't know what we're going to do about Alex, though," she added. "After you passed out, I managed to talk to my dad. He said that Alex was right, that there's never been a Devoured of chaos. There are so few Makars already and so few mages become one of the Devoured, and Makars never have before. We don't know how to stop him. We don't even know much about the Devoured. In the mage world, we don't like to admit it can happen."

Call thought of Tamara's sister, Ravan, and of Master Rufus's own teacher, Master Marcus. Both of them had become Devoured and, indeed, they were spooky. No longer quite human, not quite elemental. Call never knew whose side either of them were on, and no one seemed to know how much of their former selves remained.

Although, for what it was worth, Alex seemed exactly like the same evil, obnoxious self he'd been before he was a Devoured of chaos. Just with a lot more power.

"This is a mess," Call said. "I have no idea how to stop him."

Tamara sighed. "Me neither."

You can't tell her that, Aaron said. *Say something encouraging.*

"But I'm sure we'll think of something?" Call tried weakly.

Tamara frowned.

Say that if we work together, we'll find a way to defeat Alex. We always do.

Call repeated the words, trying to sound like he really felt that way. The way Aaron would have said them.

Tamara held up a hand. "No. Absolutely not. Why are you talking that way? The Call I know would never say that. The Call I know would be talking about packing bags and running off to a remote location where we could disguise ourselves and hide. Then later he might reluctantly do something heroic." She gazed at him with deep suspicion. "Something is going on."

Call winced and thought of his dad, who not too long ago had actually suggested they run away to a remote location. Tamara knew him alarmingly well. He couldn't put off telling her any longer.

"Uh," he said. "Aaron is in my head."

"Call, don't *lie* to me," Tamara said. "This isn't the time."

"I'm not lying, and I'm not kidding," Call said in a harsh whisper. "When Aaron died — on the battlefield — his soul passed into me. And not that sort of weird half Aaron, but real Aaron. Aaron's soul is alive and it's in my head."

Tamara looked at him with her mouth open. She was clearly trying to decide if he needed a massive dose of medicine.

Tell her you can prove it, Aaron said.

"I can prove it," Call said. "Give me a chance."

After a long hesitation, she nodded.

Let me talk, Aaron said. *Just for a minute.*

Call didn't exactly know what he meant, but he nodded. Tamara was staring at him — definitely noticing he was nodding for no reason — but Call was past caring. He needed someone to believe him that this was true. *Go ahead.*

"Tamara," he said. He hadn't meant to say it, the word had just come out of his mouth. He sat still — it was like listening to Aaron. What was he going to say next? "Remember that first night after the Iron Trial?" Aaron said.

Tamara nodded, wide-eyed.

"Call went to bed early. We were sitting in the living room and you said, 'Don't worry that he's in our apprentice group. He won't last the week.'"

She stared at him for a long moment. "You could have told Call."

It was a good sign that she was acting like she was talking to Aaron. Good, but weird. Call had given Aaron permission to control his body, but he still didn't like it.

"Okay," Aaron made Call's mouth say. "How about this? When I stayed at your house that summer, your dad kept walking around in that white robe with all the gold trim on it and one day you put it on and pretended to be him, but he caught you and he caught me laughing. Remember? I was so scared he was going to throw me out, but he just walked away and we all pretended it never happened."

"Aaron!" Tamara cried, and threw her arms around Call. She was sobbing. "It is you. I know nobody else knew that."

"I can't believe this," Call muttered. He was enjoying holding Tamara, but there was nothing about what Aaron said that he'd liked. "You both wanted to get rid of me! You suck!"

Tamara pulled back a little, her eyes shining with tears. "We got over it," she said.

Call wasn't feeling entirely over it himself yet, but he was glad she believed him. When she looked at him again, there was something new in her face, something she'd never seen before. "Call," she said. "I was wrong. You did something amazing. I don't know how you did it, but you brought Aaron back from the dead."

"And that's good," Call said, not sure of how to navigate such a weighted conversation. "Right?"

Well, obviously I think so, said Aaron.

"I keep thinking of something you said when you first came to the Magisterium, when you were just learning about the mage world. You didn't understand why the Enemy of Death was such a scary name. Do you remember what you said? *Who wants to be the Friend of Death?*"

Call did not remember saying that. He shook his head.

"I've thought about it a lot," Tamara told him. "About how there's nothing wrong with wanting no more death. We all want that. That wasn't Constantine's problem, and bringing Aaron back is so good it's incredible. It's amazing. Call, you did something no one has ever done before."

"Well, two problems," Call said, although he was reluctant to give up any of her good opinion. "One, Aaron more or less got pulled into my head by trying to keep me from being destroyed by chaos and I'm not sure we could ever do anything like it again. And, uh, two, we have to get Aaron a body."

Her eyes widened a little. "Oh, yeah."

Before they could get down to the nitty-gritty of the ethics of body stealing, Master Amaranth returned. Beside her was an Assembly member Call recognized but didn't know by name. Master Amaranth's snake had turned an aggressive orange and its head was hovering in the air over one shoulder, like it wanted to strike at the new visitor.

"Callum," said Master Amaranth. "Against my advice, key members of the Assembly have come to the Magisterium and are eager to have a meeting with you and some of your friends. You would think they would be a little more patient, but it turns out they are very bad at waiting."

The Assembly member beside her wore an increasingly pinched and unhappy expression but didn't rise to the bait. "We're sorry," he said. "But this is a matter of urgency. Alex Strike has sent us his demands and they involve both of you."

↑≈△○@

The Assembly was meeting in the large stone room around the round table where Call had sat in front of them before — most notably, when he'd brought them Constantine Madden's head in a bag. That had been a big hit, or so Call liked to think.

When he and Tamara came in, he was surprised to find Jasper already there, talking in hushed tones with one of the members. Call got close enough to hear that their conversation was about Jasper's dad, currently imprisoned in the Panopticon. If Anastasia had been sentenced to death, what was Jasper's dad's punishment? He couldn't be in really bad trouble, Call tried to reassure himself. Surely Jasper would have told them. But looking out at the unsmiling faces of the mages, a chill went through him.

"Enough, enough." A sharp voice cut through the chatter as Call and Tamara took their seats. Master Rufus seated himself opposite them, his arms folded. A few other teachers from the Magisterium were with him. "Enough. Everyone come to order," called Assemblyman Graves — ancient and grumpy, he was one of the senior voices in the Assembly. "We have business to discuss."

Everyone settled down. Call tried to catch Jasper's eye, but Jasper was staring at his own folded hands.

"We have suffered a great loss today," said Master North. "Master Rockmaple, after a long life dedicated to selfless service to his fellow mages, is dead."

"Not just dead," said Master Milagros, red-eyed. "He was sucked into chaos. Who knows where his soul may be wandering."

"He was saving two students," said Master Rufus. "He will be remembered as a hero. As should Call," he added, shooting a look at Assemblyman Graves. "If it were not for our Makar,

Alexander Strike might have succeeded in murdering even more innocents."

"And it is Alexander Strike who this meeting has been called to discuss," said Graves. He lifted a piece of paper from the stone table in front of him as if it were a distasteful object. "I have here his list of demands, which reached us after he was reportedly seen at the Panopticon, 'rescuing' Anastasia Tarquin from a very deserved punishment."

"He sent a *letter*?" Tamara whispered. "Who does that?"

"What kind of demands?" snapped Master North. The rest of the group was abuzz.

"We have no reason to give in to any demands of his!" said Master Taisuke. "He is no longer holding hostages. We should not cooperate."

"In a sense, he holds us all hostage," said Rufus. "No one knows what a Devoured of chaos can do."

"He can burn the forest," said Tamara. "He can create black holes of chaos that only Call can dismantle. And Call practically killed himself doing it."

Assemblyman Graves looked down his long nose at her. "Tamara Rajavi," he said. "I'd imagine you'd want to hear this list of demands, since it specifically mentions you. Or would you rather chatter?"

Call grabbed Tamara's hand under the table before she could climb over it and take a swing at Graves, who cleared his throat, perched a pair of glasses on his nose, and started to read.

To the mages of the Magisterium,

By now you know that I, Alexander Strike, have become a Devoured of chaos. I am chaos, and chaos is me. I can unleash the destructive power of chaos on the earth any time that I want. I can burn down cities and evaporate oceans. I can destroy the world.

You have only one chance, and that is to do whatever I say. I would consider a truce with the Magisterium if the mages are put immediately at my disposal to construct a stronghold for me. I have enclosed a drawing. It will be massive, made of marble and granite. I want it built near the Magisterium so every apprentice has to look at it whenever they're outside of the caverns, and I want it to have a big movie room and also a balcony. It must dwarf any stronghold Constantine Madden ever had.

As soon as the stronghold is constructed, I will occupy it. Then you will bring me more things I want. Deliver to me Callum Hunt, Tamara Rajavi, and Jasper deWinter, and have them bound so they can't do magic. In fact, have them gagged, especially Call. Lastly, I want Kimiya Rajavi delivered to me, though she will come willingly.

Alexander Strike.

"That's ridiculous!" said Master Taisuke the moment Graves had finished, standing up to slam his hand down on the table. "It can't really say that. It sounds like the petulant letter of a child! These aren't reasonable requests. He wants us to build him a mansion and give him — what? His enemies to punish? A girl? He wishes to play at being some kind of villain from a fable?"

"He believes my daughter Kimiya was in love with him," Mr. Rajavi said. "She is a foolish girl, but very ashamed of being led astray. Being with him again is the last thing she would wish."

Graves gave him a skeptical look but didn't comment.

"I saw Alex," Mr. Rajavi went on. "He didn't seem at all like the boy I remembered. He wore an enormous cape and seemed to delight in frightening us. All his demands might seem absurd, but he does really have power and the childishness of his desires. That, to my mind, makes them all the more frightening. A grown mind is reasonable, but a child's mind is capricious."

"A Devoured of chaos," Assemblyman Graves said after a moment. "We have no experience with such a thing, do we?"

A silence followed.

"No," he said, after letting it go several moments. "Callum, as a Makar, what do you know of this?"

Call cleared his throat and started to panic. This was the kind of situation he never did well in. He always said the wrong thing.

You don't know anything either, Aaron told him. *Just tell them that.*

"There's this lizard I know," Call said.

He could hear Aaron's groan in his head, but Call went doggedly on. "And he warned me about something else — something that had been sent into chaos. So I guess the only thing I know is that maybe Alex brought chaos elementals back with him? Like maybe that dragon."

Graves didn't seem impressed. "Could *you* become a Devoured of chaos?"

"What?" Call blurted out.

Graves adjusted his spectacles. "If you used your ability to manipulate chaos without a counterweight, you might well be drawn in and yourself made into one of the Devoured. You would be a creature of chaos, not quite human. But you might be able to take down Alex. It would be a very heroic act."

Call just stared at him. He couldn't believe Graves was really suggesting such a thing, but then he recalled the way Aaron had known they were treating him well because they were going to eventually ask him to die for them. Now Call was the only Makar in town. Unfortunately for the Assembly, Call had never been particularly good at gratitude.

You thought I was a sucker, is that it? Aaron asked.

"No!" Call said, then realized he'd answered Graves more directly than he'd intended.

"Call's correct. He's not doing that. It would be suicide," said Master Rufus, interrupting any possible objections. "Call, Jasper, Tamara — I want you to understand what's happening here, because telling you that Alex wants you delivered to him is a risk. A risk not everyone here thought we should take." He glowered at Graves, who glowered back. "Now that you know of Alex's requests, now that you know of the danger he poses to you directly, you might be justified in wanting nothing to do with it. Alex believes we'd never tell you he's asked for you as prisoners, out of fear you'd run away, but I trust you. I believe you won't run because of the death and destruction it would bring on innocent people.

"We have no plans to turn you over to Alex, but I move that we start building his stronghold, because that will make him believe we're cooperating and buy us some time. You need to use that time. Call, you are our only Makar. Reach inside yourself. Find your power. Figure out how to defeat Alex."

Everyone stared at Call.

Say you'll do your best, Aaron told him.

"If I'm going to do this on my own," said Call, in a hard voice, "if I have to figure out how to defeat Alex, even though I'm still a student, then I want something from you. Whatever I do, whatever my friends decide we need to do to destroy a Devoured of chaos, I don't want you to stand in our way. I want you to help me. Enough treating me like I'm an enemy — *the* Enemy. Understood?"

There was a silence. Master Rufus's face was unreadable; Call wondered if he'd gone too far.

Graves took his spectacles off his nose and squinted down

the table at Call. "We understand, Mr. Hunt," he said. "We understand you very well."

"Good," Call said, and stood up. To his relief, Tamara and Jasper stood up, too, clearly ready to go where he went. "Then I'll do my best."

CHAPTER NINE

CALL MADE IT all the way back to their rooms before his burst of fearlessness deserted him. They found Gwenda waiting nervously in the room for them, and there was something about the look on her anxious face that knocked the last of Call's strength. He collapsed onto the couch, face in his hands.

"I can't do this," he said. "I can't."

Tamara climbed onto the couch next to him and reached for his hand. Call noticed Jasper noticing the gesture, but didn't care. What did it matter what Jasper, or anyone, suspected about his relationship with Tamara at this point?

"We'll help you," Tamara said. He was glad she hadn't said everything would be okay. But Tamara was too smart to say that. She knew those kind of promises didn't mean anything;

she made the kind she could keep. "You won't be alone." She looked up. "Right, Jasper?"

He nodded. "Yeah. Of course."

And I'll be here, said Aaron. *Remember when it was me on this couch? Remember me throwing my shoe because I knew being the Makar meant I'd have to die for the Magisterium?*

Yeah, Call replied.

"And I'll help, too," Gwenda said, then paused. "Wait, what did I just promise to help with?"

Jasper told her quickly about the meeting, and the message from Alex.

"You mean you have to figure out how to defeat a Devoured of chaos?" Gwenda said incredulously. "Actually, wait, *we* have to figure out how to defeat a Devoured of chaos, since I just promised to help? I can't believe it. I always wondered how you got sucked into these things, Tamara and Jasper, and now I know."

"No kidding," said Jasper. "How do we wind up saying these things? Who wants to be involved in this kind of stuff?"

"You don't have to be if you don't want to," said Call.

"Don't be ridiculous," said Jasper. "Of course I do. I mean, I don't *want* to, but you get the point. What's our first move?"

"Do you think Alex has allies?" said Gwenda, sitting down on the table. "Besides Anastasia Tarquin, I guess."

"Not like Master Joseph did," said Call. "Alex isn't the Enemy of Death. He doesn't care about ending death and grief.

He only cares about power. So a lot of the people who followed Constantine and his group probably won't follow Alex."

"What was up with the dragon?" Gwenda asked. "It must have been a chaos elemental, but it was *huge*. Was that Automotones? Do you think that was what Warren was warning us about?"

"Automotones is a different huge elemental, but since Alex came back, who knows what else came with him," said Tamara. "We have to assume that even if he doesn't have *followers*, he can still control enough monsters that a direct attack would be chancy."

"No one knows how to stop a Devoured of chaos," Call said. "I mean, I don't even know much about the Devoured. Mages don't seem to like to talk about them."

Tamara sighed. "Yeah, when Ravan became one of the Devoured, my family pretended she was dead. They thought it was better that way. But when I needed her help, she was there for me. She still considered herself to be my sister."

"Is she . . . human?" Gwenda asked, looking uncomfortable.

Tamara shook her head. "She doesn't have to be human to matter."

The last time Call had seen Ravan close up she'd been ushering him and Jasper out of the Panopticon, a pillar of terrifying fire. The last time he'd seen her from a distance, she'd been helping Tamara and Jasper escape Master Joseph. She'd been a plume of flame.

Don't forget the battlefield, Aaron said. *She was there, too.*

"Alex seems like exactly the same jerk he was before," said Call. "But Ravan — wait, can you still get ahold of her?"

"What do you mean?" Tamara asked.

"We could ask Ravan about being Devoured," Call said. "About strengths and weaknesses. Maybe she could help us figure out how to defeat Alex."

"The mages are still looking for her," said Jasper. "They don't like to let Devoured just walk around loose. If they caught her, they'd bring her back to the Magisterium and lock her up again."

"We're not going to get her caught," said Call. He looked at Tamara in what he hoped was an innocently hopeful manner.

She sighed. "Yeah, I can contact her, but Jasper's right. She would be taking a chance sending back a message. She might not try."

"Everything's a long shot right now," Call said.

"In the meantime we should try to find Warren again," Gwenda said. "I bet he knows more than he's letting on."

"He *always* knows more than he's letting on," Call admitted.

"Well," said Jasper. "It's time we got it out of him. We need to interrogate that lizard. Get a bright light and tie him to a chair and tell him he will be sleeping with the fishes if he doesn't tell us everything he knows."

Tamara's eyebrows went up. "He's always sleeping with the fishes," she said. "At least he is when he's not eating them."

"We could lure him out with a plate of food," said Gwenda. "What do you think he'd like to eat?"

They debated that for a while and wound up using magic, a trip to the Refectory, a net, and a rummage through their own junk drawers to come up with a plate they were sure had something to appeal to Warren. On it were cave crickets, eyeless fish, gems, coals, and lichen that tasted like cotton candy.

The four of them, Havoc trailing behind, walked through the parts of the cave calling "Warren!" and finally set the plate down to wait.

Nothing happened. Jasper started to whistle. Gwenda started a game of tic-tac-toe with Tamara.

"The time is closer . . . !" Call said loudly, hoping the little lizard would be unable to resist finishing his favorite sentence.

"What?" Gwenda said, and then yelped as Warren scuttled out of the shadows. He made a beeline for the plate and devoured a cricket.

"Delicious," Warren said. "Many thanks for food kindly provided."

"Warren," Call said. "We need your help."

"Warren guessed that," Warren said, discarding the lichen. He snapped up a few more crickets. "You have seen the Devoured of chaos, yes? You know why Warren warned you."

"Yeah, we know," said Call.

"Though in the future we'd appreciate more concrete warnings, you know?" said Jasper, totally failing to grab

Warren and interrogate him. "Less of this beating around the bush. Just say what you mean."

The lizard regarded him darkly and ate the last cricket. "Come with Warren. I have something to show you."

"Does he always refer to himself in the third person?" Gwenda whispered as they followed Warren out into the corridor.

"Not always," said Call. "It's inconsistent."

Gwenda muttered something about not being able to believe they were doing this. It was late, and the corridors were dimmed with low light. No students were around as they hurried after the bright lizard, who turned corners so swiftly that they were soon all lost. Call could sense his companions growing uneasy as the ground slanted down and down, and the walls became more splotched with damp. He felt as if he could sense the presence of the weight of the whole mountain above him, pressing down.

They came at last to a passage that was more like a crack in the rocks. It was horribly narrow. Warren scuttled into it, clearly expecting the rest of them to follow. Havoc, unable to fit, hovered worriedly by the entrance.

Call glanced toward Tamara, who swallowed hard and slid into the space after the lizard. They had to shuffle sideways to push themselves along, the stone pressing against their backs and stomachs. Call could hear Jasper complaining that he should have eaten less lichen at dinner. *Please, please, don't let me die stuck here*, Call prayed, *and I'll do everything I can to defeat Alex.*

He heard Tamara give a gasp of relief, and a moment later he popped out of the narrow space like a cork out of a bottle.

All around them were walls made of hardened volcanic rock, black and craggy. The heat was intense. Both Jasper and Gwenda gasped as they emerged into it. Fire was audible in the distance, crackling like thunder.

"Where are we?" Jasper looked around. A wide corridor led between two long rows of cages, whose bars were made of glimmering gold carved with fire symbols. Call had been here before, though he'd come through Anastasia Tarquin's offices.

"This is where they keep the Devoured," said Tamara quietly. "Those who have been consumed by elements. This area is for fire."

"Warren?" said Call. "Warren, what are you doing? How did we get in here?"

"There is a secret way into every place," said Warren. "And someone here wants to see you."

He began to scamper down the corridor. After a moment, the four students followed. It was so hot that Call felt as if every breath were searing his lungs. Tamara and the others looked miserable, too. He was glad Havoc hadn't come — a fur coat was the last thing anyone needed down here.

Most of the cages were filled with what looked like roaring bonfires; some were blue or green, most red and gold. In one cage, lava dripped from the ceiling like fiery rain. A wheel of fire spun in the air.

Tamara paused in front of an empty cage. The inside was blackened stone. Her lip trembled. "Ravan," she said, touching the bars.

"Your sister is free." The voice crackled like fire itself — Call knew immediately who it was. The students turned to face the cage opposite them.

Marcus, Devoured of fire, sat on a burning throne inside his cage. He was all black smoke, except for two burning eyes made of fire. He had been Master Rufus's own teacher, until he had let fire control him.

Warren ran squeaking into Marcus's cage and scampered up one smoky leg. He perched on Marcus's knee as the Devoured scratched his scaly back. Warren half closed his eyes and purred. Call had seen a lot of weird things, but he had to admit this was one of the weirdest.

"Wow," Gwenda whispered.

Privately, Call agreed. He went up to the bars of the cage, as close as he could without getting burned. "Marcus, we need your help," he said. "You've helped us before."

"And to what benefit to myself?" Marcus inquired. "I am still here, inside this cage."

"You've done good in the world," Tamara said firmly. "You helped us defeat Master Joseph."

"And now his apprentice rises, more powerful than ever he was," said Marcus. "Perhaps there is no victory, Rufus's children."

"He actually only became my Master fairly recently," said Jasper. "I mean, for the record."

"Marcus," Call said firmly. "What do you know about Alex Strike? The Devoured of chaos?"

"I heard rumors such a creature had risen," said Marcus. "At first, I did not believe. To be Devoured of chaos is to be overcome by the void. That which is not. The emptiness at the heart of the whirlwind."

"Well, believe it," said Tamara. "Is Automotones back?"

"Many have returned," said Marcus. "The Devoured One was consigned to chaos. But he was able to tear open a door into our world and return. He brought with him those he thought might help him here — Azhdaha, the Great Dragon. Automotones. The most savage of the Chaos-ridden ever to be hurled into the void. All have returned at his side."

"What about Stanley?" said Jasper.

"Who the heck is Stanley?" said Gwenda. Even Marcus looked puzzled.

Call sighed. "He was a Chaos-ridden who was loyal to Constantine. Me. Whatever. I don't think Stanley was his real name either; it's just what I called him."

"*Stanley?*" said Gwenda.

"Forget him," said Tamara. "Marcus, we need to know how to kill a Devoured of chaos."

"Yes, you do," Marcus said.

Call was frustrated and sweaty. "Why did you want to see us? Warren said you got him to bring us here."

At the sound of his name, the lizard scuttled up to Marcus's shoulder and began kneading it the way a cat would, flicking his tongue out at the hot air. Call guessed they were closer than he'd thought.

"It was you who sought Warren," Marcus reminded them. "I had him lead you to me because of Rufus. Had I not become Devoured, Master Rufus might have been less distracted, less willing to allow Master Joseph to get close to Constantine. We all bear a share of the responsibility for the Enemy of Death, and I would like to discharge mine by aiding the defeat of this new threat."

"Great," Call said. "Then help me. Help *us!*"

Marcus looked at him with burning eyes. "Everything you need is already with you."

. *Does he mean me?* Aaron asked.

"That's not helping!" Call said. "Just say what you mean for once. No more riddles!"

"Good luck, mages," Marcus said, then burst into a column of flame. When it died down, no one was there but Warren, the gems on his back gleaming brighter than ever.

"I will take you home now," the little lizard said, racing ahead before waiting for a response, leaving them to scramble after him.

"That was *Master Marcus*," Gwenda said as she followed. "I can't believe you know him. I can't believe we just talked to him. He's a legend. And terrifying. A terrifying legend."

"Yeah," said Jasper, looking a little pale. "We're really cool like that."

Call's leg was hurting as he scrambled through the tunnels and he felt the opposite of cool. In front of the Assembly he'd acted like he was capable of finding a way to stop Alex. But as they headed toward the less stuffy parts of the Magisterium, he started to despair.

We're going to be fine, Aaron said, but he didn't sound entirely sure himself.

Warren paused, alighting on a rock above a wending stream that flowed through the caves. They were back in the familiar part of the Magisterium.

"The time is now," said Warren.

"Wait," said Gwenda. "I thought it was *closer than we think.*"

"The time is now," Warren repeated, then scuttled away into the shadows.

Gwenda turned to Call. "Does he always say *that*? Please tell me this is normal."

"Uh," Call said. "No."

"Forget Warren being cryptic," Tamara said, dusting off her uniform and tucking a stray strand of hair behind one ear. "Maybe we're overthinking this. Maybe what we need is a weapon."

Jasper looked back at her. "What kind of weapon?"

She gave them all a fierce look. "That's what we're going to find out."

↑ ≈ △ ○ @

A few hours later, they had covered the table, the couch, and a large chunk of the floor in their common room with books they'd borrowed from the library. Each of them had a stack and were skimming through, looking for weapons that might be useful against Alex.

It turned out that mages had made a lot of things over the years, though very few of them measured up to something like the Alkahest, which could kill chaos users with their own magic and which Alex had modified to steal Aaron's Makar abilities and which had been, thankfully, destroyed. Most were useful but kind of dull things like knives that returned to the hand of the person who threw them. A few were just weird.

"I found a hatchet that cuts the heads off three pigeons with every single throw," Jasper said, looking up from his book with a frown. "Who would want to make something like that?"

"Someone who really hates pigeons," Gwenda said with a yawn.

Just then there was a knocking on the door. Call went over and waved it open to find a bunch of First Years including Axel and the girl who'd been carried into the air by the dragon.

"We just wanted to thank you," said Axel. "Because you're awesome."

"I'm Lisa," the girl said, thrusting a drawing at Call. "We just wanted you to know that we will never believe anything bad anyone ever says about you. You're cool and you saved us and I drew a picture of it."

Call took the picture and goggled at it. He couldn't deny that it was actually very well drawn. The face really looked like him, but the body was much more built and also featured his shirt ripped open over six-pack abs. "Uh," Call said, embarrassed.

Tamara grabbed it out of his hands. "This is *amazing*," she said with enthusiasm that Call was sure came from mockery. "You're really talented. We're going to hang this on the wall."

"We are most certainly not," said Jasper, who would have loved the drawing had it been of him.

Thank them, Aaron said. *Tell her it's a great picture.*

With Celia telling people that Call was evil, he supposed he couldn't afford bad public relations. Maybe these Iron Year kids could help him get back in the good graces of the rest of the students.

"Thank you," he told Lisa. "It's great."

"It *definitely* is," Tamara agreed.

"We just wanted you to know," said Axel, "whatever you want, we're there for you. We'll help. Really, anything."

"You guys are so sweet," said Tamara.

A wicked grin grew on Call's face. Now here was a gift he knew what to do with. "Great!" he said. "As you can see, we're really busy, so how about you go to the Refectory and get us some of those lichen cakes that taste like pizza. And then I need some more books from the library —"

"Call!" Tamara said, interrupting him.

He gave her an innocent look. "Maybe just the lichen cakes for now," he said to the Iron Years.

They nodded and headed off to do Call's bidding.

"They're not your personal servants," Tamara said.

"I think you will find that they are," said Call, then admitted, "I guess I get an Evil Overlord Point for that."

"What?" Tamara asked.

"I'll tell you later," he said, realizing that maybe he didn't want her to know about the Evil Overlord list. And he definitely didn't want Jasper and Gwenda, who were looking at him oddly, to start tallying up points for him.

If there's no weapon in these books, we're going to have to get serious, Aaron said. *I know you don't want to look at the memories, but they might be our best hope of defeating Alex.*

It won't help anyone if I go full E-o-D, Call thought back. He missed the days when he believed that cheating on a test or taking the last slice of pizza was enough to make him into a bad guy. The memories were dangerous and dangerously tempting. What if he could save the world but it meant losing himself?

But if he became Constantine, would he even want to defeat Alex?

Call went back to the books, but with every page he flipped, he felt his options shrinking.

↑ ≈ △ ○ @

By the time they got through all the books, the lichen cakes were a distant memory. They were frustrated and hungry. Finally, Gwenda stood up and stretched her arms over her head.

"Okay," she said. "We need a break."

"Do you think Alex is taking a break?" Jasper demanded. "Evil never takes a break."

"Well, Gwenda's right. We need one," said Tamara. "Let's go down to the Gallery and go for a swim. We need to let our minds rest and see if we get any new ideas."

"Sugar might help," Call agreed. "Sugar and caffeine."

"Fine," said Jasper, realizing they were all against him. "But we are still not hanging that picture of Call on the wall."

"That's right," Tamara agreed. "We're hanging it on the fridge."

And she did.

↑ ≈ △ ○ @

The Gallery was surprisingly full of students. Call would have thought that after the traumatic events of the past day, especially the death of Master Rockmaple, it would have been a dark and subdued place. But it was stuffed full of people, raucously yelling and having a good time.

Tamara shrugged. "Denial," she said as he glanced around, taking in the kids jumping in and out of the hot and cold pools in the rocks. They'd put in a bunch of squishy gold velvet sofas, and a ton of students were sprawled on them, sipping drinks in bright colors: blue, green, orange, and pink. "People need to be distracted. It's normal."

Gwenda and Jasper were already over at the long stone snack bar, filling plates with candy and crunchy dried lichen flavored like nacho cheese. Call grabbed a frozen sugary tea and Tamara a glass of something with raspberries and huge lychees.

They all headed over to the squishy couches, when Call suddenly stopped short. Celia was sitting there with Charlie and Kai, wearing a flowered yellow shirt and laughing. She looked pretty and lighthearted — at least until she turned to see him, and her face went still.

"Maybe we should go somewhere else," muttered Call.

"Well, would you look who's got the nerve to show himself in here," someone said. It wasn't Celia. It was a boy in a denim shirt and swim shorts, with red hair and long skinny legs. Call thought he recognized him, but he wasn't sure.

That's Colton McCarmack, said Aaron's voice in his head. *He was friends with Jennifer Matsui, before she died.*

Call felt a cold lump in his stomach. He had brought Jen Matsui back to life as a Chaos-ridden. It hadn't been his choice to do it, but it had still been horrible.

"Look, we don't want any trouble," Call said, holding up a hand. "We'll go sit somewhere else."

"As long as you're in the Magisterium, you're trouble," said a girl sitting next to Colton. She had short black hair with bright dyed blue bangs.

Yen Ly, said Aaron. *Colton's girlfriend.*

Did you know EVERYONE in the Magisterium? Call thought with exasperation.

Just trying to help. Aaron sounded annoyed.

"You were close to Alex," said Colton, leaning forward. "Weren't you?"

"What's this about, Colton?" Tamara demanded, her hands on her hips. "Alex faked being our friend. He killed Aaron, who was Call's counterweight. Surely you're not going to suggest we're big fans of his."

"Leave Call alone." It was Kai, looking a little embarrassed. He cleared his throat. "We all saw him save those kids this afternoon. And destroy Alex Strike's chaos magic. He's obviously on our side."

"Too obviously," said Colton. "Alex had already gotten what he wanted. I figure it was all staged to make it look like Call was fighting off the Devoured, when really he's in league with him."

"'In league with him'?" echoed Jasper. "Who talks like that?"

"And you." Colton turned on Jasper. "Didn't your father join Master Joseph? You talk as though we have any reason to believe you're loyal to the mages, but somehow when Call was broken out of prison, you and Tamara were there. Tamara, whose sister Kimiya is Alex's girlfriend. Everyone knows you're both as corrupt as he is."

At the mention of his father, Jasper seemed to shrink.

Rage sprang up in Call. "Back off," he said sharply. "No

one is in league with Alex. Jasper doesn't even like me that much, and we're about to risk our lives again to save you, so unless you'd like to take my place fighting the Devoured, maybe you should leave us alone."

"Celia's right about you," Colton says. "You're not to be trusted, and anyone who can stand being around you can't be trusted either." With that, he walked off, his girlfriend and friends following.

Call and the others walked back to their rooms with heavy hearts. Gwenda, who hadn't spoken to Colton and hadn't been accused of being evil either, was probably weighing the potential benefits and drawbacks of being their friend. Call was pretty sure the math wasn't on his side.

CHAPTER TEN

W HEN HE OPENED the door with a wave of his wristband, Call saw that the wall of stone was on fire. For a moment he just blinked at it, until he saw that the fire was spelling words.

MEET IN THE PLACE AT THE HOUR OF YOUR AGE.

The letters turned to ash and then vanished, leaving nothing behind.

"More weird stuff," said Gwenda glumly.

"It's a message from Ravan," said Tamara. "She communicates with fire. It's her language. And her handwriting."

"Okay," said Jasper. "But how are we supposed to know what she means?"

"'The place' is probably the place I met her last year," Tamara said. "On the grounds of the Magisterium."

"Outside?" asked Gwenda.

Tamara nodded. "But 'the hour of your age'? Does she mean my birthday?"

"Or the time you were born?" Jasper put in. "How would you know that? Unless you call your mom or something."

Sixteen-hundred hours, Aaron said. *Military time.*

Call opened his mouth to say that Aaron had figured it out when he remembered that would be a mistake. "Four in the afternoon," he said instead. "Because she's sixteen."

"That only gives us twenty minutes!" said Gwenda, and they charged back out.

Call brought Havoc. Havoc might not be Chaos-ridden anymore, but you never knew when you might need a loyal wolf.

They raced through the corridors of the Magisterium, heading for the Mission Gate. As they left the Magisterium, Call couldn't help thinking of Alex's arrival with the dragon, especially because in the distance, his stupid tower was being built. Mages flew through the air, lifting blocks of stone with their magic, each resting on top of another as the edifice grew. It might be ridiculous, but it was being made and Call was running out of time.

"Here we are," Tamara said as they arrived in a grove. She climbed up on a rock and sat down.

For a moment, they waited, drinking in the smell of pine needles. Somewhere in the distance a wolf howled and Havoc pricked up his ears.

Then, all at once, like a spark flying up from kindling, Ravan was there.

She looked as much like a girl as Call had ever seen her. She was surrounded by a nimbus of flames, and her left hand was all fire, like a burning Alkahest. Her eyes were full of fire, too, and her hair shot sparks. But she was still girl-shaped, and, unnervingly, Call could see her resemblance to Tamara. It made him uncomfortable for reasons he couldn't articulate to himself.

Because the thought of something like that happening to Tamara freaks you out, said Aaron. *Because you like her. You're in like with her.*

Do you MIND? Call thought. *It's none of your business.*

It is as long as I'm stuck in here. Besides, I'm hoping you crazy kids make it work.

"Ravan." Tamara had stood up, appearing to understand she was the unofficial spokesperson for the group. "Thanks for coming."

"You're my sister," Ravan said, sparks flying from her mouth as she spoke. "You wanted me to come, so I came. What is it?"

Tamara reached up to fiddle with her necklace. "We need to know how to kill a Devoured."

Ravan started to laugh, which sounded like fireworks going off. Jasper scuttled back a few feet, clearly nervous that sparks were going to land on his clothes. "Why would I tell you that?"

"Because otherwise Alex Strike will kill me, and Kimiya, too," said Tamara.

Ravan stopped laughing. She hovered, burning, as Tamara explained what was going on: the building of the tower, Alex's requests, Call's inability to hurt him with chaos.

"We don't want to hurt any other Devoured," Tamara finished. "But we need to get rid of Alex, Ravan. He could kill a lot of people otherwise."

"I see," Ravan said. "I can tell you now, I have never heard of a Devoured of chaos before. A Devoured is killed the way elementals are killed — they are destroyed by their opposing element. I could be killed by a Devoured of water, or by an enormous amount of water magic, my fire put out forever." She sounded as if she were full of dread. "But chaos . . ."

"The opposite of chaos is the soul," said Call. "There's no such thing as a Devoured of the soul."

"There cannot be," said Ravan. "A person cannot be Devoured by their own soul. It would be like being murdered by life."

"Well, what are we supposed to do, then?" said Gwenda. "We can't send souls at him."

"I don't know," said Ravan. "I would help you if I could."

Tamara looked bitterly disappointed. "If you hear any other elementals or Devoured speaking about a way to get rid of Alex, please, please tell me."

"I will, little sister. Stay safe. If you need me, I will come again." And with that, Ravan burst up into a tornado of flame, whirling in the air and then dispersing into sparks as though she'd never been there.

The four of them who remained sat in silence, their hope dashed. Call's mind raced — surely there had to be some other option, some other idea, someone else they could ask. Havoc barked when one of the sparks drifted too close to his fur. Call thought even he sounded depressed.

In the distance, a howl echoed through the woods.

"What's that?" Jasper said, sitting up straight.

"It's probably one of the Chaos-ridden wolves . . ." Gwenda said, letting the sentence trail off. From the beginning of their time at the Magisterium, the woods had been full of Chaos-ridden creatures. The Order of Disorder had even moved to study them. Then the Assembly had rounded them up, and even though Call had rescued them from that fate, they weren't in the woods anymore.

"Maybe they came back," said Tamara, hopping down from the rock and walking to the edge of the woods.

Another howl came, this one much closer. Then, from the opposite direction, one of the wolves slunk into view. It was a dark shape, like it had been cut out from paper, with nothingness occupying where it should have been. The fur on Havoc's back lifted. These weren't Chaos-ridden wolves, at least not anymore. These had come back from the void with Alex and now they were chaos elementals, far more powerful and far more terrifying.

Fire ignited at the center of Tamara's palm, a ball of it that grew as she stood. Havoc bared his teeth and ran toward the beasts.

"No!" Call shouted, racing after his wolf and then stumbling. He fell painfully onto his knees as Gwenda leaped to stand beside Tamara, raising her hands. Little jagged pieces of iron and nickel began to rip their way out of the earth as Gwenda summoned metal, then flew toward the chaos creatures that were coming out of the woods from every direction.

A few howled and fell back, the metal tearing holes in their smokelike bodies. Call could see *through* their wounds into the woods beyond.

"Stand back-to-back," Jasper shouted.

Call pushed himself to his feet, ready to send these elementals back into chaos. But they'd crept too close to Tamara for him to be sure that opening a portal wouldn't pull her through the way it had Master Rockmaple.

Havoc had made it to Tamara and was standing between her and the chaos creatures, growling.

We've got to do something, said Aaron, which was not particularly encouraging.

Call sent out a bolt of chaos energy, targeted toward one of the wolves closing in on them. It disappeared, dispersed by nothing into nothing.

Two of the wolves rushed toward Gwenda from opposite directions at once and she pulled up metal to send at one of them. It struck the creature in the throat, sending it flying back. Jasper threw himself in front of the other wolf, creating an enormous snap of wind, one that broke the branches of trees behind the wolf and sent it flying against a rock.

Tamara sent fire at the wolves near her, but more gathered around. Call started to panic, shooting bolts of chaos toward the wolves. Gwenda was still flinging metal, and there were deep holes in the ground all around her, but she was starting to look desperate. She'd run out of metal eventually, Call knew. Both Tamara and Jasper were tight-faced with exhaustion.

There were too many of them, too close to Tamara, Gwenda, and Havoc. There was no way he could send them all to the void in time. One lunged for Tamara's throat, teeth snapping against her skin.

The memories, he thought in a panic. If he had Constantine's memories, he would know what to do. Constantine was the Enemy of Death. He could have handled this situation.

Call took a deep breath. *Aaron —*

Are you sure? Aaron wanted to know.

"Unlock them," Call said. "Do it."

All right.

It felt as if something inside Call's head was tearing. He dropped to his knees, clutching at his temples. Havoc ran to him, putting his paw on Call's arm; Call ducked his head, aware that fire and metal were flying all around him. His leg sent stabbing pains through him, matched by the pressure and pain in his head.

Aaron, he said. *Aaron, whatever you're doing, I don't think I can —*

The block in his mind crashed open like a gate, flooding his brain with images. He was aware of Havoc making a terrible noise, a sort of wailing bark as he leaped away from Call, cowering.

Power surged up inside Call, brutal and terrifying. He was propelled to his feet, even as the woods around him seemed to shift and waver — other memories overlapped these woods, of ancient forests deep with trees, dark paths winding through them, lined with ferocious elemental monsters.

And through all of that, Call could see something he had never seen before. Chaos, living chaos, like black lines running through the world. The sky and earth were dark with it. This was why chaos had such power, he thought — because it was a part of everything, of every rock and tree and cloud; it was in and around all things. It was the spinning heart of the world.

He reached out with his hands as if he were reaching to pick up something simple like a cup or a stone. He caught the twisting coils of chaos that wound all around him and pulled them together, weaving a massive spinning black flame between his hands.

He could hear the others screaming his name. It didn't matter. He knew exactly what he was doing. Somewhere in his mind, Aaron was shouting. Call flung his arms out, and the black flame exploded from his fingers, striking the elemental wolves, tearing them to shadowy pieces.

Jasper had flung himself in front of Gwenda and Tamara. They all watched, stunned, as the wolves blasted away to ash, and black fire raced up and down Call's arms, crackling like lightning.

"Call!" Tamara screamed. *"Call!"*

But Call couldn't hear her. He could only see and hear black fire, only remember burning. In fact, memories were pouring into his head, in an uncontrollable tide. As he tumbled down into darkness, he could hear himself screaming.

CHAPTER ELEVEN

H E **WAS IN** an ice cave. The cold of it made his breath
crystallize in the air. He could feel it even through his
heavy coat, even through his magic. There was a terrible pain
in his chest and all around him were the dead and dying.

If he didn't act quickly, he was going to be one of them.

He had come here to strike at the old and infirm, the weak,
because he knew from long experience that fear was more pal-
pable than might. It gave him no pleasure to attack the elderly,
children, sick people. Yet the person who cares the least is
always the winner and he wanted to win. He was willing to do
whatever it took, no matter how terrible, and he was willing to
do it himself, not trust it to some underling.

He'd never expected such a weak and infirm collection of
people to mount such a response. The Chaos-ridden he'd

brought with him were destroyed, fallen in their second death, and he'd been hurt. Badly hurt.

His body was failing, its heart slowing, its lungs drowning in their own blood. He cast about for a new vessel. Sarah Hunt, who'd sent the magical knives into his chest? He'd managed to turn a few of the blades back to strike her and now she leaned against the wall, mortally wounded, watching him with wary, dulling eyes. No, she wouldn't be alive much longer. He glanced at a few of the grandparents, their bodies protecting children. Dead, all of them dead.

A thin, thready cry went up, and he saw that there was a baby, still alive, held in the arms of a man — Declan Novak, Sarah's brother. Declan had slumped down against the wall near his sister. The mage made swift calculations. He had no idea whether his Makar power would go with him into this child. He'd always taken care to possess the body of a Makar before — if the power didn't go with him, then he might well find his end at last.

He took a long and painful step closer to the baby, ignoring Sarah's cries for him to keep away. The child was wailing, which was a good sign. It was still strong, a survivor, with a shock of black hair and angry waving fists.

A baby. As an infant, he wouldn't be able to do magic or leave the cave. He would be defenseless. He would have to take the chance that someone came. Worse, he was afraid that the unformed mind would be overwhelmed by the full scope of his memories. And yet, Constantine's body was fading fast. It would never last long enough for him to find another candidate.

His memories would have to be walled up inside this vulnerable new mind, he decided swiftly. It was a tidy solution in its way — only when he was a mage strong and wise enough to find those memories locked up inside his head would he be able to free them. He would receive all the wisdom he'd once possessed only when he was ready for it. After all, without his memories, how would he ever return to glory?

And he, Maugris, the Scythe of Souls, the Devourer of Men, the Enemy of Death, was intended for glory. Glory forever and ever, for all time.

Taking a deep breath, his last in this broken body, his soul pushed its way out of what was left of Constantine Madden and into the screaming infant that had been Callum Hunt.

This is not the end of me, he vowed.

↑ ≈ △ ○ @

Call woke with a scream and then went on screaming. Someone had tied him down to a bed and there were scorch marks on the wall, scorch marks Call didn't recall making. He didn't recall the walls either, or the room.

"Call?" It was Jasper's voice, and for a moment, Call quieted. He knew where he was, after all. Or at least he thought that he did before the room tilted and everything slid away.

Then it seemed to him that he was in a thousand places at once, that there were a host of people passing before him, trying to talk to him. A thousand voices shouting. Mages in Assembly robes, men and women with burned and blackened skin, shaking their fists.

"I defeated you in Prague!" Call shouted back at one of them. "It was I, and I shall defeat you again!"

"This is really not good," said Jasper's voice. Call found himself back in his body. His wrists were tied to the posts of a large bed whose hangings bore marks of punctures, water damage, and smoke. His shoulders ached.

"It's me," Call said. His voice sounded hoarse, and his throat ached. "Where's Aaron?"

I'm here, said Aaron's voice in his head. *Call, you've got to get hold of yourself. Push the memories back, wall them up again. You were right —*

Jasper looked worried. Why he was next to Call's bed, Call didn't know. "Aaron's dead," he said. "Call? Do you know where you are?" He ran to the door. "Tamara! He's talking!"

A girl raced into the room, her hair flying. Brown skin, dark hair, beautiful. Call knew her but the knowledge was rushing away from him. He gripped the ropes connected to his wrists, trying to hang on. "What's happening now?" he said. "What happened then?"

The girl — *Tamara, Tamara* — came close to his bed, her eyes full of tears. "Call, what's the last thing you remember?"

"The ice cave," Call said, and saw both of them stare at him in horror just before he tumbled off the edge of everything.

↑ ≈ △ ○ @

He was in a massive stone room. Constantine Madden was pacing back and forth in front of a huge dais made of granite, his customary mask pulled down over his scarred face. On top of the dais was a tomb, and on the tomb lay a body — one that Maugris recognized easily. He knew both Madden siblings well enough. It was Constantine's brother, Jericho.

Jericho was motionless in death but Constantine was full of movement. He raced from one end of the room to the other, the silver mask that hid half his face gleaming. Over and over he spoke to his brother, telling him that he'd bring him back, that he should never have died, that the Magisterium would pay. Death itself would be destroyed.

Maugris watched with interest. He understood hating death. He had spent generations and centuries avoiding it himself. Looking down at the elegant but wrinkled fingers of his own hand — a woman's hand this time — he knew he could easily have a decade or three more in this body. And yet Constantine, in his present state, might not last so long. He would burn up — all ambition and impulse and no strategy.

Master Joseph had done good work, separating him from the Magisterium, from the people who cared about him.

Maugris allowed himself a moment of pleasure and pride in his cultivation of that mage. A man broken enough to be manipulated, broken enough to break that child, had been an excellent choice for an apprentice. And yet he had never suspected his Master of anything but inflaming his own ambitions. He had certainly never suspected her of being a Makar. The mouth of the woman's body he wore curled up into a smile.

The last time he rose in power, the last time he had made a bid for taking a bite out of the mage world, was long enough back that they would never connect him with those who had come before. That was the value of lying low for several generations: It gave the world time to forget. But this new Makar had tried some interesting experiments. He had failed to bring back the dead, but he'd given Maugris an idea for an army. An unstoppable army.

It was time to become Constantine Madden.

This has all been and will be again.

Call opened his eyes again, back in the stone room with the bed. The scorch marks were no longer on the wall, but he wasn't sure if he'd imagined them or if they'd just been washed away. He heard howling — Havoc? Chaos wolves?

"Call?" came a soft voice. He turned his head. "Do you remember who you are now?"

Celia was there, her wispy blond hair pushed back with a headband, her face so pale that what stood out was the redness of her eyes. Call frowned at her, trying to place her in his memories. She didn't like him.

Had he burned down her tower and scorched all her lands? Murdered her family? Spit in her soup? There were so many crimes rushing through his head.

"Call?" she said again. He realized he hadn't answered.

"You . . ." he croaked, raising a finger to point accusingly at her. She'd done something, too, he remembered that.

"I'm so sorry," she said. "I know you must be wondering why I'm here when I've been so awful — and I *was* awful. I was afraid. I had family here at the Magisterium when your father — and *you*, I mean not really you, but *him*." She stopped speaking, clearly having gotten herself tangled up in her words. "When Constantine was at the school, no one thought he would become the Enemy of Death. They knew he was all puffed up about being the Makar and believed he could do things no one else could, but it didn't seem that bad. Until it did. A lot of my family died in the Mage War, and when I was growing up, they warned me over and over again about how brave I would have to be to stand up to Constantine, but that if someone had, none of this would have happened."

Murdered her family, Call thought. *That was what I did to her.*

Call, came a voice in his head, a voice that startled him. *Call, you have to focus. Push back the memories.*

"I know that's an excuse," Celia said. "But it's also an explanation, and I wanted you to have one. I was wrong, and I'm sorry."

"Why now?" he wanted to know. Why had she decided to forgive him when she'd been right all along? He wasn't trust worthy. He wasn't even sure he was Call.

"You nearly died saving Jasper," she said. "Constantine wouldn't have. Maybe he'd have done some of the other stuff to look good, but I couldn't think of any reason to do what you did other than being Jasper and Tamara and Gwenda's friend. And then I started to think about the walks we used to take with Havoc and how horrible it would be for everyone to think something bad about me for something I couldn't control. And then I thought that it wasn't fair you had to almost die for me to think better of you. And then I heard you weren't okay and I wondered if things would have been different if we hadn't — if I hadn't — "

"It wasn't that," he started, but then the room tilted again and he got a lungful of smoke. He was standing on the deck of a ship and in the distance he saw an entire armada on fire. He watched mages leaping into the sea, but when they got to the water, tentacles reached up for them out of the depths. He needed to warn her. The girl. The girl who was sorry.

"There are elementals," he told her urgently. "Under the waves. Waiting. They will drown you if you let them."

"Oh, Call," he heard her say, voice soft and broken up by sobs.

↑ ≈ △ ○ @

He was lying on a narrow wooden bed. He knew he was dying. His breaths were coming in ragged gasps and his body felt as if it were full of fire.

This was *not* what he had planned for his life. He had been a brilliant student of the best Magisterium in the empire. His teacher, Master Janusz, had been the wisest and most powerful Master, who had chosen him first at the Iron Trial. He was a Makar who could shape chaos. He had been assured of a long life of power and riches.

And then the coughing had begun. He had dismissed it at first as the product of exhaustion and long nights working in the laboratory he shared with his Master. Then, one night, the coughing had bent him double and he had seen the first red spray of blood across the floor.

Master Janusz had brought the best earth mages to heal him, but they could do nothing. His power had waned with his health, and he had become a prisoner in his garret, eating only when his landlady or Master Janusz brought him food, waiting in a fury for the inevitable.

At least until the day he realized.

He had always known it. The opposite of chaos is the soul. But he had never really, truly thought about what it meant. Since the day he had thought of it, he had lain in his bed, considering the possibilities, dwelling on method, on opportunity . . .

The door to his garret opened. It was Master Janusz. Still a man in his prime, he bustled over to the dying mage's bedside. The man in the bed hated his former master. How dare he have health and a future when he had already had so many years?

He seethed as Master Janusz fussed with his pillows and used fire magic to light the candle by his bed. The room was already growing dark. He listened as the older mage wittered on about how he would be well soon enough, as soon as the weather was warmer.

"Nonsense," he said, when he could stand it no longer. "I am going to die. You know it as well as I do."

Master Janusz paused, looking stricken. "Poor Maugris," he said. "It is a shame. You could have been a great Makar. One of the greatest the world has known. It is a shame and a pity for you to die so young."

Rage came upon Maugris. He did not want pity. "I would have been the greatest Makar history has ever known!" he roared. "The world would have trembled before me!"

It was then that Master Janusz made his mistake. He came toward the man in the bed, hands outstretched. "You must calm yourself, my boy — "

The dying mage reached out with all his strength, not of his body but of his mind. The idea that had burned inside him flared into life. He was a manipulator of chaos. Why couldn't he also manipulate the soul?

He reached within Master Janusz with hands made of smoke and nothingness, and saw the other man's eyes bulge. With all his strength, he tore his own soul free from its moorings and pushed — pushed it into Master Janusz, hearing the mage's tinny scream as his soul was forced out into nothingness. . . .

A few moments later the door burst open. The landlady, hearing the commotion, had raced upstairs. She saw before her a scene she had expected: her dying young tenant had expired, white-faced and still in his bed. Master Janusz stood in the center of the room, a dazed expression on his face.

"The boy," she said. "He died?"

The Master did a very strange thing. He grinned from ear to ear. "Yes," he said. "He is dead. But I will live forever."

↑ ≋ △ ○ @

"Aaron." It was Tamara's voice. "Aaron, I know you're in there."

Call opened his eyes. They felt like heavy weights. Celia had gone, if she had really been there in the first place. Tamara was sitting next to his bed. She was holding one of his hands.

But it was kind of strange that she was calling him Aaron. He was pretty sure that he wasn't Aaron. Except he wasn't entirely sure he wasn't. Memories swirled inside his head — a Chaos-ridden wolf puppy, a burning tower, a monster made of metal, a room full of mages, and he was one of them. One by one he killed them all, so they could never go against him. He watched them fall and laughed. . . .

"I was the Scythe of Souls," he croaked. "I was the Hooded Kestrel, Ludmilla of Prague, the Scourge of Luxembourg, the

Commander of the Void. I was the one who burned down the towers of the world, who parted the sea, and death will die before I do!"

Tamara made a choked noise. "Aaron," she said. "I know you're in there. I know Constantine is doing this somehow. He's driving Call out of his mind."

It's not Constantine. The words swirled up inside Call's mind. He didn't quite know what they meant, but they carried an enormous urgency with them. He found words spilling from his mouth suddenly:

"It's not Constantine," he gasped. "There's another mage. One even more evil and way more ancient. His memories were blocked up, but we unblocked them and they're basically blowing up Call's brain."

Tamara's eyes widened. "Aaron," she breathed. Her body jerked forward. "Aaron, you have to save Call. You have to close those memories off! Wall them up! And Call — you have to help him. You have to let him do it."

For a moment, it seemed as though he'd fallen back into the morass of memories, that time slipped and went sideways again, but then there came another feeling, like a cool cloth against his brow. It was the feeling when someone came into your mess of a room and put everything away when you were gone, but in the right places, in the places you'd meant to put things.

"Aaron?" Call said. He was able to separate himself from the torrent again.

I'm here, came Aaron's voice. *Do you know who you are?*

"Yes," Call said. From the end of the bed, Tamara was watching him warily, clearly reserving judgment as to whether Call talking to himself out loud was a good sign or a bad one.

And who exactly is that? Aaron asked, sounding as though he was coaxing a cat.

"Callum Hunt." He turned toward Tamara. "I'm okay now. I know I'm Callum Hunt. I remember — well, I remember a lot."

She let out her breath all at once and sagged against the footboard of his bed.

"How long was I . . . like that?" His stomach growled. It had seemed both instantaneous and endless, the cascade of memories. He could feel them still, at the edges of his mind, whispering.

"Five days," Tamara said, and Call gaped at her.

"Days?" he repeated.

"Let me bring you some food," she told him, and rose. He caught her wrist on the way to the door.

"I have to tell you some things," he said quickly.

She smiled a soft smile that was at odds with her usual fierceness. "Later," she told him, and he was too exhausted and wrung-out to protest. He watched her walk out the door, then slowly and painfully pulled himself into a sitting position. His whole body ached, his leg the worst of all.

In his memories, in those other bodies, his leg hadn't hurt. But he didn't miss the feeling. It had been horrible, being that evil, deathless mage. And being caught in those memories had felt like drowning, gasping for consciousness the way he might have gasped for air. He didn't know how Aaron had controlled them.

Are you okay? he asked Aaron. And then, because they were alone, and he wanted to know: *Are you afraid?*

Yes, Aaron said. For a long moment, there was only silence in Call's head. *And yes.*

Tamara came back carrying plates of lichen and fizzy sweet drinks. Gwenda and Jasper followed her, carrying even more food — sandwiches, pizza — and setting it up where Call could get to it easily without getting out of bed. Soon his blanket was covered with platters of food.

Tamara went back to the door as Gwenda and Jasper sat down near Call. "Okay, we're supposed to tell Master Rufus that you're awake, but we wanted to talk to you before we did," she said in a low voice. Then she snapped her fingers. "And someone else wants to see you, too."

Havoc trotted in. He seemed a little subdued and looked nervously at Call. For a wolf, he had a great side-eye.

"Hey, boy," Call said in a hoarse voice, remembering how Havoc had flinched away from him in the forest. "Hey, Havoc."

Havoc trotted up and sniffed Call's hand. Apparently satisfied, he lay down on the floor and stuck his paws in the air.

"Master Rufus thinks you were sick from using too much chaos magic," said Jasper, but he sounded dubious. That was probably because he'd heard Call raving about his memories and burning down cities.

"That's not what happened," Call said. No one looked that surprised. Gwenda took a sandwich and nibbled the edge. "Look, I have to tell you something and I promise it's the last secret I will ever have. Like if it even seems like another secret is coming my way, I will dodge and weave to avoid it."

Liar, some part of him said. Some part of him that wasn't Aaron, but that he couldn't hide from Aaron. After all, Gwenda and Jasper still didn't know there were two souls inside of him. But at least he had told Tamara. At least he wouldn't have any secrets from her.

"Okaaaaay," said Gwenda slowly. "So did you remember being Constantine?"

"Kind of," said Call. "But I remember being someone else, too."

"Like past lives?" Jasper asked.

"Exactly like past lives if instead of reincarnation, you imagine me as a mage who learned how to push the souls out of living people and put his own soul inside instead."

"Like body-hopping?" Gwenda said, wrinkling up her nose.

"Exactly," said Call. "Now imagine he only body-hops from Makar to Makar because he doesn't want to lose his chaos powers. Imagine him — me — shoving the soul out of Makars through history and then becoming different Evil Overlords."

"How many?" asked Tamara.

Gwenda got up and started toward the door. Call sighed. He supposed he should have expected that.

"Where are you going?" asked Jasper, and Call wanted to tell him to shut up, not to make Gwenda say whatever awful thing she was thinking, because Call didn't need to hear it. But Call didn't tell Jasper to shut up because he didn't want Jasper to leave, too. He especially didn't want Tamara to follow them out.

But Gwenda came back a moment later with a big book called *Makars Through History.* "Okay," she said, eyes sparkling. "Were you the Monster of Morvonia?"

"I don't think so, actually," Call said. "Doesn't ring a bell."

"I guess it's good you weren't *every* evil mage throughout history," said Tamara.

"The Hooded Kestrel?" Gwenda asked.

"I was that one," he answered. "Unfortunately."

Her eyebrows went up. Tamara bent to see the page Gwenda was reading from. "Yikes," she said. "It says here that he used to use his chaos to churn up his victims' insides. Gross. Like a magical egg beater."

"Do you mind?" said Jasper. "I'm eating lichen."

"What about Ludmilla of Prague?" said Gwenda.

Call nodded. "I was definitely her."

"She sent a plague of beetles against the men of Prague when one of them divorced a friend of hers." Gwenda chuckled.

"No approving of the Evil Overlords," said Jasper. He turned to Call. "Look," he said, "we've been through a lot together. So much so that I can say that I don't really care which evil magician you were in your past life."

"Lives," Call corrected gloomily.

"Water under the bridge," said Jasper.

"But you *were* Constantine Madden," said Gwenda. "Right?"

"I was, but it's complicated. It looks like the original evil mage, Maugris, tracked Constantine down *after* he'd become the Enemy of Death. He jumped into his body, and no one ever noticed the difference, probably because Constantine was already pretty evil. It does explain, though, why he never really tried to raise Jericho from the dead after that, just moved him to a mausoleum — Maugris didn't care."

Tamara shuddered. "I can't imagine having someone else's memories thrust at me all at once like that. No wonder you were so disoriented."

Tell me about it, said Aaron.

Call nodded. He very deliberately didn't say that if his soul had started out in someone named Maugris, then those memories didn't belong to someone else. They belonged to him, even if he wished they didn't. "There was one thing, though," he said. "I — I mean Maugris — was around for a really long time. And he saw some stuff. Like another Devoured of chaos."

For a moment, they were all quiet, looking at him.

"Seriously?" Gwenda said. "You're not just messing around? Maugris saw a Devoured of chaos?"

Call nodded.

"Do you know how to stop Alex?" Tamara asked, looking as though she was holding her breath.

"I have a way," he said. "Maugris managed to purify the chaos out of the Devoured he fought. According to the rules of alchemy, it took four Devoureds of four different elements to do it. But if we can pull the chaos out of Alex's body, then we can fight him normally."

I wish I could fight him, Aaron said. *I wish I could punch him right in the face.*

"So he'd live?" Tamara asked. Call couldn't tell if she was disappointed or not.

Call nodded. "Maybe if he'd been Devoured longer, then there wouldn't be as much of him left, but I think he will be strong enough to be dangerous. Remember, he's still a Makar."

"So he could do it, too," said Jasper. "He could push out someone's soul. He could jump into another body when he was dying, just like Maugris."

Call started. "But he doesn't know he could do that."

"Come on, Call. Think like an Evil Overlord," said Jasper. "He knows what Constantine Madden did. He knows how he survived the Cold Massacre."

Tamara nodded. "Jasper is right. We're going to have to be very careful."

In Call's head, the beginning of an idea bloomed.

"At least we have a plan," said Gwenda, picking up a fizzy drink and taking a big gulp. "I thought we were never going to come up with one. This is pretty exciting, actually."

Jasper shook his head, as though mourning the reasonable Gwenda of days past.

↑ ≈ △ ○ @

Call thought that after all the being unconscious and raving that he wouldn't be able to sleep, but it turned out that after eating and talking, he was exhausted. Whatever the visions had been, they weren't restful. Luckily that night he didn't remember his dreams.

At the bell, he rose, stretched, scratched Havoc, and went out into the common room. Master Rufus was there, waiting for him.

"Callum," he said. "I am relieved to see you up and moving. We were all afraid for you, an altogether too common occurrence these days. Since Aaron's death, you've been taking far too many risks. How many times have you overextended your magic? How many times have you done magic that would be dangerous even if you had a counterweight, which you don't."

Call looked down at the floor.

"Choose another counterweight and do it soon. No, that person won't be Aaron, but they will keep you alive."

Call still didn't speak.

Master Rufus gave a long sigh. "I can't tell you to be more careful, not when the Assembly is sending you up against Alex. But if this is about guilt —"

"It's not," Call said quickly.

Master Rufus put his hand on Call's shoulder. "Aaron's death was never your fault."

Call nodded uncomfortably.

He's right, said Aaron.

"None of this is your fault, Call. That would be like blaming yourself for being born." Master Rufus waited a moment, as though expecting Call to reply, but he didn't.

"I've been thinking," Master Rufus went on. "About my own situation. About how one has to sometimes face uncomfortable things."

"Are you going to tell your husband?" Call said. "About being a mage?"

The older man gave a rueful smile. "If we get through this, yes."

There was a knock on the door. Master Rufus went to answer it, swinging the door wide. On the other side was Alastair.

He looked haggard and drawn, as if he hadn't slept in a few days. His hair was rumpled. "Call!" he exclaimed, pushing past his old teacher. He reached Call and seized him in a hug.

"Your father has been very worried about you," said Master Rufus, when Alastair stopped thumping Call on the shoulder blades and stood back to look at him. "He's been staying in the Magisterium since you first fell ill."

"I thought I heard your voice," Call said, remembering his dad's words tangled up among the flood of other memories and visitors.

Alastair cleared his throat. "Rufus, could Call and I have some time alone?"

"Certainly." Polite as always, Rufus showed himself out.

Alastair and Call sat down on the sofa while Havoc trotted over to investigate. After nosing at Alastair's pant leg, he curled up and fell asleep on his shoe.

"All right, Call," Alastair said. "I know this wasn't the flu or something like that. What happened to you? You were shouting about burning down cities and marching ahead of armies. Is this something to do with the Enemy?"

Be careful what you tell him, Aaron warned as Call opened his mouth. *If he thinks you're in danger, he'll drag the whole Magisterium into it.*

He was right, Call knew. So he told his father an edited version of events: that Constantine's memories had been walled up in his head, that he had let them loose when he'd thought he needed to save his friends, that they'd overwhelmed him until he'd gotten control and shut them back down again.

Alastair was already half out of his seat. "I don't like the sound of this. We should get Master Rufus — surely there's something the mages here can do to make sure those memories either stay put or are removed forever."

No, Aaron warned. *If they start fiddling around in here, there's no telling what might happen.*

"Wait," Call said. "What did they tell you? Did they tell you about Alex Strike?"

"The boy who came back as a Devoured of chaos? Yes, but . . ."

"Did they tell you they expect me to figure out how to defeat him?"

Alastair sank back onto the couch. "You? But you're just a kid."

"I'm the only Makar they have," said Call. "And no one knows how to defeat a Devoured of chaos."

Alastair looked at him in horror. "My car is parked outside," he said in a low voice. "We could run, Call. You don't have to stay here. We could lose ourselves easily out in the normal world."

"But then," said Call, "I think a lot of people would die."

"But *you would live*," said Alastair, intensity in his gaze. It made Call feel good to know that Alastair put Call's life above everything else in the world, but the only thing that would make Call different from Constantine or from Maugris was if he didn't.

Again he remembered the Cinquain, the line he'd added: *Call wants to live.* Again and again he'd thought about it, ashamed. Now that line seemed to cut to the heart of the terrible desire that had led him to become a monster.

Okay, several different monsters.

Call, Aaron said. *Everyone wants to live.*

And everyone deserved to live. Even if that meant Call put his own life at risk.

"I really have to try," he told his father. "And I even have a plan. It just — I need some Devoureds to help me. I know a Devoured of fire, but I need three others, for the other three elements."

"And what happens to them?" asked Alastair.

Call shook his head. "They un-Devour him. Regurgitate him. Get him puked up from chaos. And then they wind up being in the same danger the rest of us will be in, fighting a really angry regurgitated Makar."

Alastair blinked a few times. Finally, he shook his head and spoke. "Yeah, I know a guy."

"You do?"

"Up in Niagara. He was in the war. That was when he got Devoured. He might listen if we put the case to him."

"Can you drive?" Call asked.

"What?" Alastair said. "Right now?"

"Right now." Call stood up and started to wake his friends by banging loudly on their doors.

CHAPTER TWELVE

A N   H O U R   L A T E R   the Phantom was flying up the interstate with Havoc's head hanging out the window, pink tongue flapping in the breeze. Call was in the front seat with Havoc while Tamara, Gwenda, and Jasper sat in the back.

They'd stopped for fast food already and torn through a box of chicken. Cold sodas were balanced on their laps.

"Even better than lichen," Jasper had said blissfully, gnawing on a drumstick.

The radio was tuned to some jazz station. Call tipped back his head and started thinking about the future. Once Alex was defeated, he would ask Tamara out on a date, a real date. She liked sushi, so they'd go somewhere for a big fish dinner. Then maybe they'd go for a movie or a walk, get ice cream. He started to idly picture it when he realized he wasn't alone in his head. Quickly, he tried to think of something else.

He'd like to get Havoc a new leash. Yeah, that was good.

And me a new body, Aaron reminded him. *If you ever want to kiss Tamara again without me being there, too.*

Call sighed.

"You're all good kids, helping Callum out," Alastair said, which made Call feel humiliated and also about seven years old.

Tamara grinned. "Someone's got to try to convince him to stay out of trouble."

"Someone should," said Jasper. "Too bad that someone isn't you."

Gwenda knocked him on the shoulder. "Why are you the way you are?"

"People love me," Jasper said.

"So how's Celia?" Gwenda wanted to know. Jasper scowled. "Still mad at you for being friends with Call?"

"We'll work it out," said Jasper.

"I hear she didn't like that your father was in prison for helping the Enemy either," said Gwenda, and shrugged when everyone stared at her. "What? I hear things."

"We will work things out," Jasper said, tight-lipped.

"I don't think I like this Celia," said Alastair.

"She came to visit me while I was sick, actually," said Call. "And apologized."

"She *did*?" Tamara was round-eyed.

Jasper seemed relieved. "I told you."

Gwenda chuckled. "She apologized to Call," she said. "Maybe she can date *him*."

"But —" Tamara said.

Jasper looked at her with innocent eyes. "But what?"

"Nothing." Tamara crossed her arms and stared out the window. It was getting dark, and there was almost no one else on the road. The GPS showed that they were in Pennsylvania, near the Allegheny National Forest. Tall spiky trees lined the road.

Alastair cut a sideways, amused glance at Call but said nothing, and the conversation turned to other things. Call stayed quiet, thinking through what lay ahead of them.

After another half an hour, Alastair pulled off the road into a motel that had a diner attached to it. Neon promised cherry pie and cheesesteak. Call and the others followed Alastair inside as he checked them all into separate rooms and told them to meet outside in forty-five minutes for dinner.

Call was just pulling on a new shirt and doing his best to stick down his unruly hair with water when there was a knock on the door.

It was Jasper, wearing a T-shirt that read ANGRY UNICORNS NEED LOVE, TOO. Call blinked at him. "What?"

Jasper strolled in and sat down on the bed. Call sighed. In his memory, Jasper had never waited to be invited anywhere.

"Is this about Celia?" Call said.

"No," Jasper said, after a pause. "It's about my dad."

"Your dad?"

His dad's still in the Panopticon with all the others who joined Master Joseph, said Aaron helpfully.

I know! Call said. *I just don't know why he wants to talk to me about it.*

Maybe he thinks you have a sympathetic face.

Jasper went on. "One of the Assembly members told me that they're considering putting all the mages who sided with Master Joseph to death."

Call gaped. "I —"

Jasper waved his hand impatiently. "You don't have to care. It's just that we're going on this big mission to help out the Magisterium. And if we succeed, you'll be a hero." He crossed his arms over his chest. "If that happens, I want you to intercede with the Assembly. They'll do whatever you want. Tell them to let my dad go."

For a moment, Call felt that odd sensation of the world tilting sideways again, but it wasn't because an evil mage's memories were getting tangled up with his own. It was because this wasn't supposed to be his role.

He wasn't a hero. Jasper wasn't supposed to ask him for favors or act like he was important.

That was Aaron. It was supposed to be Aaron.

Hey, came the voice in his head. *I'm good with it not being me. I was good with it not being me back then, but there was no one else. And now there's no one else but you.*

Call nodded. "If we do this mission, you'll be a hero, too. You could ask them yourself."

Jasper's look was dubious. "Just say you'll do it. You're the Makar."

"I can't tell them to release your dad, but I can insist that they don't give him the death penalty no matter how his trial goes," said Call. "And I can insist he has a trial, a fair one."

For a moment, Jasper was silent. Then he gave a long sigh. "Promise?"

"I promise. Do you want to spit-shake on it?"

Jasper made a face. "No, I trust you. Besides, that's disgusting."

Call grinned, glad Jasper was acting normal around him. Together, they walked toward the diner attached to the motel. Alastair was already there with Gwenda and Tamara, sitting in a booth. They'd even gotten their drinks: Alastair was drinking coffee and the girls had milk shakes.

The overhead lighting was flickering and yellow. The linoleum was worn and cracked. But behind the case, there were pristine, glistening pies and top hat–high cakes topped with cherries and coconut flakes. Call's mouth started to water.

Jasper sat down on Gwenda and Tamara's side, leaving Call to sit with Alastair. Tamara grinned at him as he slid in across from her.

The waitress came back and took their order. Jasper got an orange soda and an enormous burger with bacon. Tamara got a tuna fish sandwich. Gwenda got a gyro. Alastair got steak and eggs. Call ordered a ham steak, a single pancake with chocolate chips, and french fries. Then he ordered two more hamburgers to go, rare, for Havoc.

"Got some news," said Alastair. "I checked in with Master Rufus on the tornado phone. Alex's tower is close to being finished. They think they can stall him, but only for three more days. Master Rufus said that we needed to complete our mission by then."

"*Three more days?*" Call squeaked. "How are we going to find three Devoureds that fast?"

"Let's just focus on the task in front of us," said Alastair. "Convince Lucas and maybe he can send us in the direction of some other Devoureds."

"But what if he can't?" Call asked, which was admittedly not the most heroic thing to say.

"You really think this plan will work?" Alastair asked.

Call nodded.

"Then we'll find a way," his dad reassured him.

Their food came, but even though it looked delicious, Call couldn't taste it.

That night he tossed and turned on the bed, sleeping only in fits and starts. Havoc licked his face, letting him know that the wolf was there with him. It helped, but he woke up over and over anyway, coming full awake as dawn was cresting outside the window.

It was time to go to Niagara Falls.

↑ ≈ △ ○ @

A few hours later, nursing an enormous cup of coffee, Call piled into Alastair's Rolls-Royce. There was less chatter today in the car and more nervous tension. Everyone seemed stressed, and when they stopped for lunch at McDonald's, even Jasper could only eat five hamburgers and a bag of fries.

After a few hours, everyone in the car had nodded off except Havoc, Call, and Alastair. "I'm sorry," Alastair said, peering into the rearview mirror to make sure the others were asleep. "I shouldn't have suggested running away, back at the Magisterium."

Call was startled. "You're the one who was right," he said. "Way back when. I never should have gone to the Magisterium at all."

Alastair shook his head. "No, Master Joseph would have found us eventually. I was sticking my head in the sand. I was wrong. You wouldn't have known how to protect yourself from him. You might have died, along with all the people you've saved."

Call fell silent. He thought of himself as fighting the evil inside him so often, he never stopped to consider any good he might have done.

The road went on and on. Eventually Call dozed off. He was awoken at a gas station by the smells of coffee and microwaved cinnamon buns. He drank some of the coffee, stretched, went to the restroom, and decided against washing his face with the slightly brownish water coming from the tap.

Back in the car, he drank more coffee and ate three glazed

cinnamon buns. By the time they arrived at the parking area of Niagara Falls State Park, he was ready to buzz off his seat like a hummingbird from the sugar.

They found a place to put the car and proceeded on foot, ignoring the aquarium and the other fun stuff, to head straight for the visitors' center. There, they got the explanation that they could go to the observation tower and from there, if they wanted, they could take an elevator down to the bottom of Niagara Falls and go on a boat ride. There was even a place called "the crow's nest" where they were pretty sure to get mist right in the face.

Call had wondered if the elevator would be made of glass, but it was ordinary metal. When they reached the bottom, the doors opened on a torrent of noise. They hurried out onto the deck. They could see tourists walking back and forth on red wooden decks, clad in bright yellow ponchos. The decks were connected by wooden walkways leading up and down.

The falls poured down so close that Call was awestruck, even though they weren't there to sightsee. As the water hit the rocks at the bottom, it exploded into white mist, then ran in torrents over the boulders past the falls and rushed away at incredible speed.

"Come on," said Alastair in a low voice. "Follow me."

He led them down several walkways as they ducked among tourists in ponchos. They were all getting wet in the down-pour, and Call's leg was starting to hurt. Alastair moved purposefully to the edge of a deck and beckoned them close, then climbed nimbly over. He helped Call over next — it was a short drop — and the others, even Havoc, landed quickly beside them.

They were on a narrow path that led by the water. Something about the path told Call it was a mage path, something invisible to normal eyes. Maybe the fact that no one else was on it. Maybe the fact that the only footprints in the dirt weren't footprints at all, but stamps that looked as if they were in the shape of the symbol for the element of water.

The sun had come out, and it dried them as they made their way along the path, the noise of the river drowning out any conversation that wasn't shouting. Alastair stopped at a place where the path jutted out into the water in a small promontory. He cupped his hands around his mouth. "Lucas!" he shouted. "Lucas, can you hear me?"

Tamara suddenly gasped. "Look!" she yelled. "There! A kid is drowning!"

She pointed.

A boy in a yellow poncho had slipped somehow, even with all the precautions and the railing. He'd fallen into the torrent frothing over the rocks and was being carried along, spun around like a leaf. For a moment he disappeared underwater and bobbed to the surface. Call couldn't tell if he was conscious or not, couldn't tell how hard he'd hit the rocks.

"We have to do something," Tamara said, rushing to the water's edge.

"Try to pick him up. Jasper and I will concentrate on calming the water. Gwenda, you make sure none of the people notice," said Call.

Jasper nodded. Gwenda scrunched up her face in concentration. She intensified the fog of the spray, creating a mist that hid them. Then she intensified two of the rainbows so that they were beautiful enough to distract onlookers. It might not be enough to keep his family from noticing what was happening, but it might mean no one else was looking.

Call had never been particularly good with water magic, but he reached out with it now, trying to control the flow of the rapids to clear a path for Tamara. He saw Jasper was concentrating on slowing the movement of water close to the boy, who was slowly rising in the air and floating toward them.

The boy opened his eyes and looked at them, but when he did, Call saw that his eyes were full of water. Tamara's magic brought him closer, but the nearer he got, the less he looked like a boy. His skin rippled and became translucent, as though he wasn't made of flesh at all. Then he collapsed into a puddle, leaving no child at all, just a yellow jacket.

"What?" Jasper demanded.

A geyser shot out of the water — and out of that came a manlike shape. "You've passed my test," he said in a gurgling voice. "Now what do you want?"

"You recognize me, don't you, Lucas?" asked Alastair.

"Alastair Hunt." The man was translucent, but the water formed a clear picture of his features, even the sketchy outlines of curly hair. "It's been a long time."

"This is my son and his friends. We need a favor," Alastair said.

"A favor?"

"We need your help. There's a Devoured of chaos and he wants to take Constantine Madden's place, fighting the mage world."

"He wants to hurt a lot of people," said Jasper. "Maybe wipe out humanity."

"And what can I do about that?" asked Lucas.

"If you were to stand with three other Devoureds, you'd be able to strip away his chaos," said Call. "He will return to being just a mage and we could fight him. Dad told me you fought in the war. Alex is the last of Constantine's minions with any power. Once he's defeated, the war can finally be over."

"That was when I was human," said the Devoured. "But I am human no longer."

"You could live anywhere," said Tamara. "But you choose here."

"I like Niagara. I like the power of the waterfall, the rush of the water."

"And the people," said Tamara. "You could be out at sea, far from anyone. You could be in one of the great rivers. You could even pick a remote waterfall. But no, you pick a place where there will always be humans nearby. And you tested us by showing us a human child in danger. I think that, whatever you are, you still care about people."

"Perhaps I do." Lucas spun slowly in the water. Gwenda and Jasper watched in wonder. "I find that I do not like the idea of humanity being wiped out. I will help you."

Call's shoulders sagged in relief. "Great," he said. "Do you know any other Devoureds? Like, of other elements?"

Lucas frowned. "This does not sound like a well thought-out plan."

"We already have Ravan, Devoured of fire, on our side," said Tamara quickly. "We just need a Devoured of earth and a Devoured of air."

Lucas made a thoughtful noise like splashing water. "Maybe Greta," he said. "Last I heard, she had taken up residence in a sinkhole near Tampa."

"Greta Kuzminski?" said Alastair. "She became a Devoured of earth? Was that because she likes dirt or hates people?"

"Mostly she hates people," said Lucas. "She was betrayed by the Assembly. They were willing to say anything to get her on their side in the war against Constantine, but after the truce, they betrayed all the promises they'd made. I'll tell you exactly where to find her, but you may have difficulty convincing her the way you convinced me."

"Great," muttered Gwenda. "I knew this was too easy."

"You don't know *another* Devoured of earth, do you?" said Jasper. "Someone friendlier?"

"I do not," said Lucas. True to his word, he gave them detailed directions, which Call tried to memorize. "Good luck to you. When you have collected everything you need, touch water and speak my name. I will be summoned to you."

With that, he melted away into the water, turning to foam and mist.

$$\uparrow \approx \triangle \bigcirc @$$

By the time they all made it back to Alastair's car, Tamara was wringing out her braids, and Call felt as if his soaked clothes weighed a hundred pounds. After glancing around to make sure no one was looking, Tamara summoned up enough fire magic to create a miniature bonfire they could all warm themselves with. (Except for Havoc, who just bounced around shaking the water off his fur.)

"So who's Greta?" Call asked Alastair. "Old girlfriend or something?"

"Just a crabby classmate. I guess things don't change." Alastair, holding his hands out to the bonfire, looked absent. "It's too bad she's all the way in Tampa. It's a long drive for you to make."

"Don't you mean it's a long drive for *us*?" said Call, surprised.

Alastair shook his head. "I think I've got a lead on a Devoured of air, but there isn't time for us to travel together if we're going to make it back to the Magisterium in time.

You just make sure to convince Greta and I'll meet you there."

"You want me to take the car?" Call asked. Alastair's Phantom was his most beloved possession; he took care of it every weekend, polishing and tinkering. Call couldn't believe Alastair would trust him with it.

"Just treat her kindly," said Alastair, taking out his wallet and peeling off a bunch of twenties, then reaching into his pocket to pull out the keys. "You're a good driver and a good kid. You're going to be fine."

Call looked at the keys and money in his hands. He thought about suggesting they fly, but he knew their own magic would only take them so far. And they didn't have time to find an elemental that could take them. "What are you going to do?"

"I've got a friend who can give me a ride. Don't worry. I'll be at the Magisterium with a Devoured of air by the time you get there." Alastair clapped a hand on Call's back, then, changing his mind, pulled him into a fierce, brief hug. "This is almost over."

Letting him go, Alastair waved to the other kids. Whistling, he walked through the parking lot, heading toward the road.

"You think he can really convince a Devoured of air?" Gwenda asked.

"We better hope so," Call said, sliding into the driver's side of the Rolls-Royce. He put his hands on the wheel. The last time he'd been sitting in this seat was when he was a little kid, pretending to drive, making *vroom–vroom* noises.

Tamara took shotgun, leaving Gwenda to sit with Havoc and Jasper.

He turned the key and pressed his foot to the gas, starting the car.

Remember when I had to drive because you didn't know how, Aaron said.

I'm still not sure I know how, Call thought back.

Tamara fiddled with the radio while Call carefully steered out of the parking lot and toward the road.

"You have your license, right?" Gwenda asked him.

"Provisionally," he said.

"What does that mean?" she wanted to know, looking worried.

"It's a provisional license," he said. "I haven't had a lot of practice, what with being imprisoned and then kidnapped and then nearly dying and then living in a cave."

That did not seem to calm Gwenda, but Jasper didn't seem worried. He petted Havoc and looked out the window.

"I like road trips," he said, watching the landscape roll by. "And road-trip games. We should play one of those."

Gwenda punched him in the shoulder.

"Ow!" he yelled.

"Punchbuggy." She smiled. "What? I thought you liked road-trip games."

He reached over and tickled her under her arms, sending her into fits of laughter as she squirmed away. Havoc barked and tried to relocate himself.

"Gwenda is so great," Call told Tamara, looking at them in the rearview mirror. "Finally someone who dislikes Jasper even more than I do."

Tamara rolled her eyes, like he was not only wrong but also maybe an idiot. Since Call had no idea what he'd said that was so stupid and didn't want to admit it, he kept his eyes on the road.

Maybe she was jealous. Maybe she didn't want to hear him compliment another girl. But Tamara didn't look particularly uncomfortable. She was leaned against the window, hair in a tidy French braid, watching the cars go by, a small smile on her face.

A few hours later, though, no one was smiling. They were bored and restless and hungry. The route took them back the way they'd come, through Pennsylvania again, then through West Virginia, Virginia, North and South Carolina, and finally through Georgia to Florida itself. It would take nearly a full day — eighteen hours — to get there. Call figured they could break it up into two long days of driving with another hotel in between.

Eventually he pulled into the parking lot of a Taco Bell. The Rolls gave a little shudder when it turned off that made Call nervous. He hoped he wouldn't have to repair the notoriously finicky car on his own.

"My butt is numb," said Tamara, climbing out "Let's grab food to take away and go find somewhere to sleep."

They were all starving, and wound up staggering back to the car laden down with sodas and bags of tacos. Jasper tried to use his phone to find them a hotel, and there was a lot of yelling and Call driving the wrong direction and then having to make U-turns. Eventually they made it to a Red Roof Inn and Jasper used his dad's credit card to book them three rooms, which was all that was available.

"Tamara and Gwenda can share," he announced, "and Call and I will each have our own room."

There was a chorus of discontent, but Jasper pointed out that he had paid for the rooms, so he got his own, and if one of the girls wanted to sleep in the room with Call, it was their business. In the end, they wound up eating cold tacos and nachos in the courtyard of the motel as the sun set in the distance.

That night Call lay in bed for a long time trying to sleep. Everything felt like a weight on his shoulders. It was hard to stay focused when he knew that he was the reason they were all there, and he was the reason they had to fight Alex, and he was the reason pretty much everything bad in the world had ever happened.

Which was only sort of an exaggeration.

That's not true, said Aaron.

There was a knock on the door. Call dragged himself out of bed, wondering if Jasper was here to ask for another favor. But it wasn't Jasper. It was Tamara.

"Can I come in?" she said nervously. She was in pajamas and fuzzy slippers. The peach color of the pajamas made her skin shine.

"I, uh," said Call.

Oh, just say yes, said Aaron irritably.

"Sure," said Call, standing aside to let Tamara pass. He was glad he'd worn his less ratty sweatpants and a clean T-shirt. And that he'd showered about five times, because he still felt gross after being soaked at Niagara.

Tamara came in and sat down on the edge of the bed. So far on the edge actually that she looked like she was about to topple off. "Call," she said, fiddling with her necklace. "Look, I wanted to talk to you about —"

"Will you be my girlfriend?" Call blurted.

Oh, no, not now, Aaron groaned.

"Shut up," Call said.

Tamara raised her eyebrows. "I know you're talking to Aaron," she said. "Maybe we should wait to have this conversation until we're alone."

Oh, go on, Aaron said. *I don't have anything else to do.*

"Aaron says he doesn't have anything else to do anyway," said Call.

"I'm not sure this is romantic," said Tamara.

"But that's the thing," said Call. "You know me. You have since the beginning, and you always see the best in me. Even though I've been seventeen different evil mages."

Eighteen, said Aaron. *But who's counting?*

"You know the truth about me," said Call. "All the truth. Everything no one else but Aaron knows. And you've still always — well, maybe not right at first — believed in me. You make me want to do good things, Tamara. You make me want to save people just to make you happy."

"But not because you actually want to save them?" she asked.

Call had the feeling maybe his speech had gone a little awry. "Kind of. Sometimes?" he answered. "Other times I wish someone else would do it."

"Fair," she said, and smiled. "Proceed."

"Well, I want to go out with you. I know I've brought a lot of weird stuff into your life and am currently possessed by our best friend, not to mention the whole Enemy of Death thing, so I get why you might be fed up with me. But in case you're not, in case you were wondering how I felt, I want you to be my girlfriend."

Tamara's smile faltered a little. "Call, I really like you."

Uh-oh, said Aaron, which did not improve Call's spirits.

"It's okay," Call interrupted her, because if he already knew the answer, he didn't need to hear her say it. "You don't have to say anything now. Just think about it. You can tell me after we deal with Alex."

She was quiet for a long, heart-wrenching moment and then let out her breath in a rush. "Are you sure you want to wait?"

Call nodded his head and gave a mock yawn. "We should probably get some sleep," he said.

Tamara leaned forward and kissed him on the cheek, making him feel overheated and confused all at once. When she went out, he experienced a pang of regret. Maybe he should call her back and hear whatever terrible thing she was going to say.

But he didn't.

He didn't sleep much either.

CHAPTER THIRTEEN

FLORIDA WAS HOT and sticky. The Rolls didn't have air-conditioning, so they kept the windows down and fanned themselves a lot. They drove past Tallahassee to a stretch of swamp near the Sopchoppy River, where Lucas had said Greta made her home.

Call turned onto the road that the GPS on Jasper's phone told him to turn on, but he did it with great trepidation. It was unpaved and bumpy and entirely unsuited to an ancient, elegant car.

The road ran along the river, which was coffee colored and smooth. All around were cypress trees, hanging with moss. The roots stretched out into the water like fingers. A snake — Call thought it might be a copperhead — swam casually along through a cluster of lily pads, past something Call thought might be the nose of a gator.

The road was quickly turning to mud and the path was becoming a lot less clear.

"You're sure this is the way?" Call asked.

"Maybe?" said Jasper. "The GPS seems to be asking us to turn again, but there isn't a turn."

The Rolls slowed, partly because Call had pressed on the brakes and partly because the mud was getting deeper. Call had the uncomfortable sensation that the car was sinking a little in the muck.

"We should get out," Tamara said. "Now."

"This car can't get stuck here," said Call. "Dad will kill me if I don't bring back his car."

"Do we even know where we are?" asked Gwenda.

"My phone knows," said Jasper. "But maybe we better go on foot from here."

They all piled out of the Rolls, feet sliding. As they stepped away from the car, it seemed to be sucked down a little more.

"Is that quicksand?" asked Tamara.

"Augh!" said Call, holding his head. "I thought quicksand was just in movies. Bad movies. I didn't think it was real."

"We can get it out with magic," Gwenda reminded him. The tires had almost entirely disappeared. "Everyone, concentrate."

Gwenda, Jasper, and Call all drew on air magic while Tamara drew on earth. Call focused on wind pushing up the car, on it forming an almost solid sheet getting between mud and metal. With a gross, sucking sound, the car bounced up out of the swamp, was pushed a few feet onto the remains of the dirt road, and then unceremoniously *dropped* as they withdrew their magic.

The clang and grind of metal as the Rolls hit the ground made Call wince. Would it still run? How many dents had they just made along the base?

There was no time to worry about that now.

"This way," said Jasper, holding up his phone. They followed him along the trail beside the Sopchoppy River, listening to the buzz of insects, grunting frogs, and the constant trill of birds above them.

The wet heat was heavy on their backs, and mosquitoes blew in clouds, making their high-pitched keening noise. Call had the uncharitable thought that maybe Lucas had sent them on a fool's errand. Maybe there was no Greta.

Jasper stopped. He shook his phone.

"What's the matter?" asked Tamara.

He shook it again. "No signal."

"You've got to be kidding me," Gwenda told him. "Now what? Are we close? Do you have any idea where we're meant to be going?"

"Over there," Jasper said, waving vaguely across the water, toward a copse of trees.

"Greta!" yelled Call, causing a few birds to take off from nearby branches. At least one of them was, alarmingly, a buzzard. "We're sorry to bother you, but Lucas said you could maybe help us!"

There was no answer. Call felt defeated, as though he'd let them all down. Although really, it had been Jasper with the phone who'd messed things up. Call opened his mouth to point that out.

Don't, said Aaron. *There's no time to blame one another. Besides, I bet he already feels bad.*

Call frowned and looked over at Jasper, who was still waving around his phone. He looked fine. But Call supposed Aaron was right.

"We could swim across the river," Jasper suggested.

"No way," said Gwenda. "That water is full of alligators. I guarantee it."

"We could fly across," Call said. "See if we can see anything."

Just then, there was a rippling in the surface of the river. They all stopped and stared.

They were standing at a bend. The water itself was a muddy gray-brown. Tall cypress trees lined the banks.

"Maybe it's an alligator," said Gwenda nervously. "Sometimes they climb up on the bank and eat people."

"Why do you know so much about alligators?" Jasper demanded.

"Because I hate them!" she said. "They're like dinosaurs with massive teeth and — what is *that*?"

The ripples in the water had become a whirlpool, swirling

around the cypresses growing out of the river. Suddenly there was a loud sucking, crashing noise, like a volcano erupting inward. The trees began to sink into the water.

"It's a sinkhole," said Tamara. "I've seen videos of them. Back up!"

They all backed away, watching in amazement as the trees and the earth at the edge of the riverbank were dragged down into the opening sinkhole with a loud, sickening noise. The trees crunched and shattered, branches snapping off as they were dragged below the surface of the water. The surface of the water roiled, and out of it emerged something huge.

It was a giant made entirely of dirt and mud. Call's mouth fell open as the creature rose above them, shedding flopping fish and huge worms. A stench rolled across the swamp like rotting garbage as the giant opened two massive mud-brown eyes.

"She's trying to scare us off," Tamara hissed as the others reeled back, gagging. "Lucas said she hates people."

"It's working," Jasper said, wiping at his watering eyes. "I'm scared."

"Go away, mages," Greta said. Her voice rolled and boomed. More mud fell off and plopped into the swamp.

Call cleared his throat. "It's nice to meet you," he called. "The, ah, mud and worms are very cool, very, ah, powerful-looking."

Greta reached out and snapped a tree in half.

"That's gonna be your spine," muttered Jasper.

Flattery won't work, Aaron said. *But I bet she's not thrilled with the Assembly.*

"Look," Call said, "we're sorry to bother you. But we don't have a choice. We need your help."

Greta blinked. Mud cascaded into the water. "Why would I want to help you?"

"We know the Magisterium abandoned you during the war," said Call. "Left you to become Devoured and then cast you out."

Greta nodded.

"There's a Devoured of chaos out there," said Call. "His name is Alex. The Magisterium is building him a huge golden tower, and in a few days we're all going to be delivered to him so he can kill us."

"That's not true," Tamara hissed, then paused. "Actually, I guess it's technically true."

"Why should I care?" said Greta, but she spoke more thoughtfully now. "What have mages ever done for me?"

"Two other Devoured are helping us," said Gwenda. "Ravan of fire and Lucas of water."

"The Assembly would have to acknowledge what you did," added Call. "They would be ashamed of the way they treated you."

Greta made a low rumbling noise. Call realized the terrible stench had gone, and Greta was looking slightly different — she was no longer shedding worms and fish. Instead, flowers were growing up and down the ridges of her rocky body, along with brightly colored mushrooms.

"The Assembly must admit its shame," said Greta. "We are the Devoured, not elementals. We are mages. We should not be kept imprisoned nor treated as monsters."

"This would be a way to show that the Devoured aren't monsters. That they can also save people," said Call. "And if Alex isn't stopped, there's no telling what he might destroy. He could wreck the whole world — and that would affect you, too, and other Devoured."

Greta rumbled thoughtfully. "Does the Devoured of chaos like frogs?"

They were all silent. Would it be better or worse if he did?

I think you should go with no, said Aaron. *Alex doesn't really like anything.*

"He probably wants them destroyed," said Call.

"Then he ought to be stopped," said Greta. "I like frogs. They're my friends."

"Tell us how to summon you," said Call. "I promise we'll only do it when all the Devoured are united and it's time to fight Alex."

Something wormed its way up from the ground between Call's feet. A shimmering geode-like hunk of quartz.

"Smash that on a rock," said Greta, "and I will come to where you are." She swatted lazily at something in the water — an alligator, its green, spike-toothed head sticking briefly out of the water. "I will expect to see the shame of all mages."

As she sank back below the water, Jasper expelled a breath. "I hope this was a good idea."

"We didn't die," said Gwenda. "That has to count for something."

They made it back to the Rolls without being attacked by alligators or frogs or an enormous pit opening up beneath them. The car had not been sucked down into another sinkhole. Even better, when Call turned the ignition, the car came to a shuddering start. It didn't sound the same as it had when Alastair had let him borrow it, but it moved well enough to allow them to drive out the dirt path.

Once they got on the highway, a whine in the car — in something that Call thought might be the fan — became more pronounced. He drove on, sending a little cooling magic toward the engine in case he was right.

They drove north, muddy, bug-bitten, and exhausted. They stopped for more fast food on the border of Virginia and made it to the caves of the Magisterium that night.

The golden tower loomed high in the sky. In the moonlight, it looked finished already.

They had one more day. One more day before he was going to face Alex again.

Call parked Alastair's car in a corner of a clearing near the front gates. He and Havoc and the other apprentices went inside, too tired to even talk. He was planning on taking a bath, but once they got to their rooms, Call fell asleep right on his bed, with mud still crusted on his jeans.

CHAPTER FOURTEEN

IN THE MORNING, Call washed up and, butterflies in his stomach, went to the Refectory to eat breakfast. Tamara, Jasper, and Gwenda went with him.

"I thought your dad was going to meet you back at the Magisterium," Jasper said.

"I'm sure he will," Call told him, trying to put faith in it. Maybe Alastair was here already. They'd gotten in late; maybe he was staying in another part of the school. Maybe they just hadn't seen him.

Call piled his plate with mushrooms and lichen but after he sat down, he wasn't sure he could eat any of it. He was worried about confronting Alex, worried about giving what he promised to Greta, worried about everything.

That was when Colton McCarmack strode up to their table, red hair bright as a new penny. Two of his friends followed, but they stopped before they were too close. "We were taking bets on whether you all ran off."

"I hope you didn't lose too much money," Call said. "Wait — actually, I hope you did." He should have been upset about Colton coming to bother him, but when Call was nervous, he got testy, and it helped to have someone to vent that testiness on.

"We were all talking and we remember how Alex used to be. Cool. A nice guy. He would have never done anything like this." Colton sneered.

Tamara gave him a look so scathing that Call was surprised Colton's hair didn't catch on fire without any magic being involved.

"Why don't you go talk to your old pal Alex then?" said Call, standing. "If you're such good friends, maybe he can make you his number one minion."

Jasper laughed.

Colton looked more incensed. "If he is the way you say, I know you had something to do with it. You did something to him. You corrupted him. You're the evil one."

"Oh, stop it," Celia said, walking over to them and putting her arm on Colton's. "Call is doing a brave thing tomorrow."

Colton gave her a look. "Not you, too," he said, and stomped off.

"Good luck," said Celia to Call softly, and then followed Colton, with a single weird look in Jasper's direction.

"What was that about?" Tamara asked.

Jasper shrugged, looking embarrassed. "She came to see me this morning. Maybe we're not going to work it out."

Call was too distracted to make sense of Jasper's love life. He was thinking of Alex, of the way he'd thought of him as friendly and funny and nice. He'd thought Alex was a good person, like Aaron. But all of that had been surface, acting. In his soul, Alex had been terrible the whole time.

We all thought he was nice, Aaron said. *That's what he wanted us to think.*

Of course, Call had an evil soul, too. And maybe Colton was right about Call's villainous ways, because he suddenly knew how he was going to win. And it wasn't a plan that anyone could describe as good.

"Tamara," he said, "can I talk to you for a second?"

Just then, Master Rufus walked up to their table. "I'm relieved you're all back. I got a message from Call's father that he's delayed. He'll be here tomorrow. But today, the Assembly wants to see you. All of you. They want to go over the final plan. If you're done with breakfast, come with me."

Tamara, Gwenda, and Jasper stood. As they followed Master Rufus out of the Refectory, Call put his hand on Tamara's arm.

Are you sure about this? Aaron asked.

"I need to tell you something," Call said to her. "Because we're not going to have any secrets."

On the way to the Assembly, he whispered to her, explaining

the whole thing he'd thought out. She didn't contradict him, even when he thought she would. She didn't tell him it was wrong.

All she asked was, "Do you think it will work?"

"I hope so," Call said, and they walked in to face the Assembly.

↑ ≈ △ ○ @

The Assembly always looked serious. Now they looked like they were at a funeral. Call looked up and down the long wooden table, recognizing faces — the Masters of the Magisterium, people from important families like the Rajavis, and Graves presiding over it all.

"Mr. Hunt," said Graves, gesturing for Call and Tamara to come and stand before the table. It was on a raised dais, so the Assembly looked down on them, some impassively, some with pity. "We understand you've been orchestrating a plan."

"That's right," Call told him, trying to project all the authority that he'd never thought of himself as having. "We're going to pull Alex back from chaos."

"You think you can make him un-Devoured?" said Master Milagros. "That's never been done."

"Actually, it has," said Call. "It requires four Devoured, representing each of the other elements."

"And you want us to provide you Devoured from our cells?" said Graves. "That's impossible."

"You don't need to," Tamara cut in angrily. "We've already assembled our own team."

"Though you did promise you'd cooperate with us and help us," Call added.

"We promised not to stand in your way," said Graves. "And we have not."

"Then you'd better not now," said Call. "Because this whole plan depends on me and Tamara and Jasper doing what you want. And in exchange, we want something."

"What is it?" said Master North.

"We want to let Alex Strike live," said Call.

A murmur ran through the room. Call heard *traitor* and *never* and, as always, *enemy*. Anger swelled inside him, and he let himself feel it. It was better than being afraid.

I'm not who you think I am, he thought at the Assembly. *I'm worse.*

Tamara spoke over the hubbub. "We've learned that maybe Alex isn't in control of himself. Maybe he is in thrall to someone else. Maybe he never *chose* to do any of those things."

Jasper whipped his head toward Call. Gwenda frowned. So did Master Rufus. All of them clearly wanted to interrupt, but they didn't.

"Who could he possibly have been in thrall to?" Graves wanted to know. "We all saw him on the battlefield. We all saw him lead an army of the Chaos-ridden. And had he been in thrall to Master Joseph, the spell would have ended when Joseph died."

Call took a deep breath. "His stepmother, Anastasia Tarquin."

They all goggled, looking around at one another. Anastasia Tarquin had been one of them, an Assembly member. It was only after the last battle that they'd discovered her betrayal and realized who she truly was — the mother of Constantine Madden, working behind the scenes to help Master Joseph get hold of Call, in the hopes Call would remember his past.

"All we want is for you to agree that if he's defeated and it turns out that he wasn't acting on his own, he won't be thrown in the Panopticon," said Call. "I know what it's like to be misjudged. I know what it's like for people to think you're evil when circumstances pushed you in that direction and you didn't have any good choices."

"And you really believe that of Alex?" Master Rufus's expressive eyebrows were raised.

"I know what it's like to feel like you can't go back, that you have no hope of a second chance." Call tried to look his most sympathetic and heroic, but he was afraid that what he actually looked like was someone bugging out his eyes. On the other hand, he couldn't look more bug-eyed than Jasper did.

"If you believe you can defeat Alex and leave him alive," said Graves, "then you believe he can be taken prisoner?"

"That is ridiculous," said Mr. Rajavi, staring in disbelief. "He will still be an out-of-control Makar — "

"No, he won't," said Call quickly. "Stripping him of all chaos will strip his Makar powers, too. He'll be an ordinary mage."

Graves shook his head slowly. "This is madness."

"Think of what he knows," said Tamara suddenly. "All Master Joseph's magic, Anastasia's secrets. If he died and we never learned any of those things . . ."

Graves's eyes sparked. "You understand," he said, "that if he seems rebellious or resistant, we will have to kill him."

"Of course," Call said. "We get it. We just think there's a good person in there, trapped under Anastasia's commands."

"Once he's been subdued, we will have to have him come before the Assembly and give an accounting of all of his misdeeds and Anastasia's role in them. Then we will decide what to believe," said Graves.

"I understand," said Call. "Thank you. But there's one more thing. I want you to change your policy on the Devoured."

"You can't be serious!" Master North said.

"I am," said Call. "If they're going to help us defeat Alex here, then they're going to want to be treated fairly. Not like criminals and monsters."

"Most of them live quietly among the elements," Jasper added suddenly. "No one's saying you shouldn't arrest a Devoured who does something wrong, but it's wrong to assume that they're evil without giving them a chance."

"This is about your sister," said Graves, staring narrowly at Tamara. "Isn't it?"

"Ravan is a good example," she said stubbornly. "She's never done anything wrong."

Jasper coughed a cough that sounded like *jailbreak*. Call and Tamara ignored him.

"She helped defeat Master Joseph," said Tamara. "And for that, she's being hunted."

"She's dangerous," said Graves.

"Many things are dangerous," Mrs. Rajavi said, voice dry. Her husband looked at her as though there was something he wished to communicate, but she was looking straight ahead. "Although the Assembly may conclude that my decision is biased, I would like to say that knowing Ravan has revealed to me that though the Devoured are not as they were, they are not elementals either. We should treat them better and we might find better allies in them."

Graves cleared his throat. "This is most irregular."

Call waited, unwilling to back down.

"We will discuss and inform you of our decision," Graves finally said, unhappily. "And now we want to wish the three of you good luck tomorrow. We stand ready to assist you once Alex is . . . subdued. We will be there, shields in place, to make sure that Alex cannot call on any more creatures of chaos. We will be witness to your bravery."

But we're not going to be coming to help you. "Uh, thanks," said Call. "Great. And when we're done, we're going to come back and discuss our reward."

"*Reward?*" Graves sputtered. "What reward?"

"We'll let you know," Call promised, grinning in Jasper's

direction. If they managed the rest of this, getting Jasper's dad out of prison was going to be a cakewalk.

Then, together, they left the Assembly. As they did, Call heard Master Rufus getting grilled and felt a little bit bad. But it was hard to feel too guilty when he was still so nervous about his plan coming together.

"What was all that back there?" Gwenda asked.

"What do you mean?" Call asked innocently.

"You really think Alex is being controlled by someone else?" She put a hand on her hip and gave him the sort of look you give someone when you believe you can tell if they're lying by some physical tic. Call hoped that wasn't true.

"Maybe," he said.

"Fine," she said. "Don't tell me. I'm going back to the room. Jasper, come on." She stomped off. Surprisingly, Jasper followed without comment.

Tamara sighed, looking guilty.

You know we're not done, right? Aaron said in Call's head.

What do you mean? Call asked.

Well, you're not going to like it, but there's one more person you're going to have to get on board.

Who? Call asked, although he had a bad feeling he already knew.

Anastasia Tarquin. You have to convince her to back up your story.

She's not going to do that.

Call explained to Tamara about Anastasia Tarquin and how Aaron thought they should contact her. "But I don't even know how to do that."

"We should call her," said Tamara. "On the tornado phone."

"That can't work!" Call said. "Alex is probably off doing evil with her. I don't think she's just hanging around, waiting for phone calls."

"Well, if it doesn't, then we'll try something else," Tamara said, changing direction and heading toward Rufus's office.

I don't want to do this, he thought. *I never know what to say to her.*

Look, said Aaron, *I was in foster care for a while. I know how to talk to people who want you to call them Mom.*

Call couldn't dispute that. He followed Tamara to Rufus's office, a path that took them along the underground river. He remembered the first time he, Tamara, and Aaron had ever traveled on this river together. They'd been in a boat with Rufus, and had watched in wonder as Rufus had summoned water elementals to propel the boat along. Call remembered the sound of Tamara and Aaron's laughter bouncing off the cave walls.

Misty water-colored memories of the way we were, said Aaron.

Call snorted. They'd reached Master Rufus's office, and Tamara held the door open so he could follow her in. The tornado phone was on Rufus's desk, and for the first time Call noticed a photograph propped up next to it of Rufus standing with his arm around a man wearing gold-rimmed glasses. He looked like a nice guy, the sort who might own a bookstore or a movie theater. Call wondered how he was going to feel when he found out he was married to a secret magical ninja.

Tamara put her hand on the glass containing the whirling tornado of the phone. "Anastasia Tarquin," she said.

The smoke inside the glass spun and coalesced. Call saw the outlines of what looked like a modern loft — a big space with lots of wood and chrome and big windows looking out onto what he guessed was New York City. Anastasia, standing at a big metal sink, looked up in surprise as the smoke focused on her face.

"Who is it?" she hissed, glancing around.

"It's me. Callum Hunt."

Anastasia's expression changed. She hesitated, then said, "It isn't safe to talk. He could be back any second."

"She means Alex," Tamara muttered.

Tell her you missed her, said Aaron.

"I missed you," Call said. She wasn't going to believe it, he thought. He'd refused to visit her in prison. But her expression softened.

"Meet me at the abandoned village of the Order," she said. "We can talk there." In the distance came the sound of a door opening. She waved her hand frantically at them. "Go! I'll see you in an hour!"

Tamara took her hand off the glass and the image inside spun away to smoke, but not before Call caught a glimpse of Alex walking into the loft. He seemed to radiate darkness, even through the mechanism of the phone.

"I feel gross," Call said, staring at the smoke.

"Not as gross as we're going to feel after we talk with her," said Tamara matter-of-factly. "The village is pretty far away — we should get going."

"I don't think you should come," Call said, knowing she wasn't going to like that.

"Of course I'm coming," she said. "Don't be ridiculous."

"This could be a trap," Call said. "I don't *think* it is. I believe she meant what she said, but Anastasia could decide that she needs to keep me safe by kidnapping me again. That's always a possibility."

"Then I'll be there to help you get away," Tamara said.

"But if Anastasia does come, she's going to be more likely to be convinced if I'm by myself." Call sighed. He didn't want to go alone any more than Tamara wanted him to, but he knew he should.

At least you'll have me, Aaron said.

"Fine," Tamara said. "I won't go all the way with you, but I am going to stand at the top of the ridge and make sure nothing happens. If Anastasia does kidnap you or betray you, at least I can let people know. At least we can come after you."

Call sighed. "Okay."

He still felt rotten.

They snuck out through the Mission Gate. When they passed other students on the way out, Call noticed there was some whispering, but it didn't seem bad. They weren't frowning and didn't look scared. They looked like Call once had, watching older students head out on an important mission.

They walked together through the woods, Tamara taking Call's hand when one of them had to cross over a rocky portion or jump over a log. Call thought of the night she'd come to his hotel room, about the conversation they'd almost had. Maybe he should say something? But maybe this wasn't the best time to bring up Their Relationship, since there was every possibility Anastasia was going to try to pop his head off with wind magic the moment he saw her.

He was still trying to think of what to say when they came to the ridge.

Tamara leaned over and kissed his cheek. "For luck," she said to his surprised expression. "Good luck to Aaron, too. You'll do great."

Which was a little weird, but still made him happy to hear. "If you hear a terrified, reedy scream, that will be me," Call said, then headed down the hill.

Anastasia was already standing in what was left of the Order of Disorder's village, an air elemental floating behind her. The houses looked even more dilapidated and the land even more overgrown than it had the last time they were here, when they'd fought Alex and Aaron had died. It was unnerving to be in the same place again, with the players in such similar positions.

You're telling me, said Aaron. There was a jitteriness in his voice that worried Call. They were in the place Aaron had died, after all. He tried to push the thought away so Aaron wouldn't have to share it.

Anastasia smiled when Call came into view and he smiled back at her. He tried to feel sympathy. After all, she loved Constantine, despite everything he'd done. She loved him enough to bring him to the Magisterium and to work behind the scenes to make sure he was safe, even after he'd become a monster and another person entirely.

She loved Constantine sort of the way Alastair had loved Call, except that Call didn't think that Alastair would have put up with quite so much of all the Enemy of Death stuff. But maybe he was wrong. Maybe Alastair would have loved him even if he was an Evil Overlord.

Call wasn't sure what he wanted to believe. But it did make him feel a little bit bad for Anastasia.

Tell her we unlocked some memories, Aaron said. *Just don't tell her which ones. Tell her you're sorry you didn't remember her before.*

"I have something to tell you, Anastasia," he said.

She looked at him with a mixture of hesitation and hope.

"I really didn't remember you, and I'm sorry," he said. "But I realized after Alex came here that Constantine had locked away his memories inside my head. He was worried a baby wouldn't be able to withstand an adult's memories. He arranged it so I wouldn't remember until I was ready."

"And you were ready?" Anastasia demanded.

"I guess," Call said. "We were attacked by wolves, and the memories just opened up. I could see myself pacing back and forth in front of Jericho's tomb."

Tell her you could see her. Aaron's tone was firm.

"I could see you, Mom," Call said. "I know how much you loved me and how much you cared about what happened to me."

Anastasia's face began to crumble. Her carefully applied makeup ran as her tears streamed down her cheeks.

Tell her it's not her fault.

"Nothing that happened to me was your fault," Call said.

"Oh, Con," she gasped, and threw herself at him, seizing him up in a tight embrace. Call dug his heels into the soft dirt to keep from being yanked off his feet. He was as tall as Anastasia, but she had the strength of hysteria.

"I need your help now, though," Call said.

Not so impatient. Kindly.

"Please," Call added. "It's about Alex."

She drew back from him, troubled. "I know he's very angry," she said. "He blames you and he shouldn't. He doesn't understand that you didn't remember. I'm sure when you explain it to him —"

Explain it to Alex? Call choked back a laugh.

"I won't be able to do that," he said. "The Magisterium has set it up so that Alex and I are going to have to fight. They want me to kill him."

"Savages!" Anastasia's face darkened. "To force brother to fight brother."

She can't seriously think of us as brothers.

You can't contradict her, said Aaron. *Make her understand the danger. You and Alex could both die.*

"You know how strong I am," Call said, trying to look at her the way Constantine would have. "If Alex and I fight, we'll kill each other."

She looked fearful. "He is a Devoured of chaos."

"I don't think either of us will survive. That's why I need your help."

"We could run away," she said. "All three of us. Live together, me and my two sons." She looked at him mistily.

"Not as long as Alex is a Devoured of chaos," said Call. "Think of it as a disease we have to cure. As long as the chaos is eating him up, he'll hate me, and then one day he'll start to hate you."

"The Devoured cannot be cured," Anastasia protested.

"They can." Call tried to project confidence and assuredness as Aaron spoke to him silently. "I've set it all up. The Magisterium insists we meet in combat, and I know how to draw the chaos out of him. Once that happens, we'll be all right — as long as you tell them Alex only ever did the bad things he did because you asked him to."

"Because I asked him to?" She drew back. "How will that help?"

"It's what they think anyway," said Call.

Don't tell her they think it because you told them so

Call ignored that. "They need to believe it wasn't him. Otherwise they'll track him to the ends of the earth and execute him. But you can take the blame and escape."

Tell her it isn't really blame. Tell her she'll be a hero. So many people will think she did the right thing.

Call took a deep breath. "A lot of people don't agree with the mage world's decisions about things," he said. "The way they kill Makar in Europe. The way they treat the Devoured. The way they blamed Constantine when all he — all *I* — was trying to do was to end death and suffering."

Anastasia nodded, her eyes fixed on his. Call felt as if he was giving the most important speech of his life.

"I'm sure that when you stand up and speak, many will sympathize," said Call. "And you can flee on your air elemental. You can make sure it's standing by."

Tell her about the future, Aaron said.

"The Magisterium will pardon Alex," Call said. "And then we'll come to you, and we'll leave the mage world behind. We can spend our lives traveling." He thought of the similar words Alastair had spoken to him when he'd begged him to leave the Magisterium. "We can be together."

Anastasia's cool gray eyes glowed. "Very well," she said slowly. "You'd better fill me in on exactly how this plan is going to go."

CHAPTER FIFTEEN

CALL FELT GUILTY as he walked up the hill. When he saw Tamara at the top, his expression was bleak.

"Did it not work?" she asked him.

"It worked," he said. "I was just thinking how maybe I understand why people are afraid of chaos mages. Maybe they *should* be afraid."

Tamara put his hand on Call's shoulder. "It's not fair that because you're a Makar, you have to deal with all this. It wasn't fair when it was Aaron, and it's not fair when it's you. We're still kids. Maybe not kids like we were when we came to the Magisterium, but too young to be responsible for the lives of so many other people. I think you're doing great."

"If you think so, then I guess it must be true," Call said.

This is my fault, Aaron said.

No, it's not, Call thought back. *This time it's not any of our faults.*

Tamara took his hand and held it all the way back to the Mission Gate. When they came through, Jasper and Gwenda were waiting for them, looking grave.

"What happened?" Call demanded loudly, cutting through the other voices. Gwenda looked abruptly apologetic and a cold sliver of fear ran through him.

"You better come," said Jasper. "Now."

He started moving through the tunnels fast enough that Call had to ask him to slow down twice just to keep up. When they arrived back at their common room, Master Rufus was there, looking very grave.

Beside him was a Devoured of air. He appeared in the form of a grayish mist that moved out from the shape of his body to evaporate in the air. His features became more and less distinct as the cloudlike shape of his body shifted.

Call could see his glasses, the shape of his face, even the translucent outline of gray-and-brown hair. Call knew him. He didn't want to, but he did.

The Devoured was Alastair, his father.

For a moment, Call's bad leg almost gave out. He lurched sideways and caught himself on a table. All Call's thoughts had fled. He didn't want to believe what he was looking at. He didn't want to see what was in front of him. He didn't want to comprehend it.

"Dad," he said. The word came out broken.

Tamara gasped.

He must really love you, said Aaron, which seemed all wrong to Call at the same time that it was true.

"Dad," he said again, and the shape flowed toward him, enveloped him in fog and whirling wind. There was nothing comforting in that touch. It was too inhuman, too cold.

"Call," Alastair's voice said. "I'm sorry. But this is the only way I could help you."

"We could have found someone else," Call pleaded.

"There wasn't time," Alastair told him.

"But you hate magic!" Call shouted, angry now. It wasn't fair. It wasn't fair that Alastair had to sacrifice himself. None of this was fair, none of it had ever been fair, but Alastair shouldn't have had to give up everything. "How are you going to go to garage sales now? How are you going to tinker with cars? How are you going to even drive cars? What is going to happen to all your antiques?" He choked. "What about our life together? What about *our life*?"

"I needed to help you, Call," said Alastair. "There's no life for me if anything happens to you. You're my son."

"And you're his father!" Tamara said. "You shouldn't have done this! Call needs you."

"This wasn't what I wanted either," Alastair said. "I will

miss going to movies, working on cars together, walking Havoc, being father and son. Being part of his life as he gets older and marries, bouncing a grandchild on my knee."

Tamara looked stricken.

"Maybe this is the price I have to pay for not having told Call the truth about magic for all those years," said Alastair. "For every time I didn't trust him. We have to trust the people we love."

"Now it's even more important that the Assembly change its rules on the Devoured," said Jasper somberly. "So Alastair can be with Call sometimes, and Tamara, so you can see Ravan."

"Ravan." She gave a little gasp. "We have to summon her and the others. Aren't we supposed to be at Alex's tower at dawn?"

"Alastair." Master Rufus spoke in a rumbling voice. "It is a noble thing you have done. Noble and painful. Even if the Magisterium does not, I will do all I can to help you after this."

"Thank you, old teacher," said Alastair. "I will be waiting for you all outside the Mission Gate at dawn."

He dissolved into the air and vanished. Call slumped down at the table. He didn't care about Alex right then. He didn't care about anything but his father. He couldn't think about anything but Alastair and how Alastair was both *fine* and *totally not at all never again going to be fine.* He felt numb all over. Numb and strange.

"Tamara, Gwenda, Jasper," said Rufus. "Go and get yourself ready for tomorrow. New uniforms have been laid out for you. They have spells that repel dark magic woven into the fabric."

I didn't know you could do that, Aaron marveled.

"Callum, stay here a moment," said Rufus. "I want a word with you."

The others left, Tamara reluctantly; Call could tell she wanted to stay with him. He'd have to get ready, too. They were supposed to leave first thing in the morning. But he felt as if he couldn't drag himself to his feet. Somehow what Alastair had done had been the last straw.

"Call," said Master Rufus, "I need you to know something."

Call looked up.

"I have had many students over the years," Master Rufus continued. "Some of the best who have ever come out of the Magisterium. And some of the worst."

Call stared dully. He waited for Master Rufus to tell him what a disappointment he was.

"I know I have not always been there when you needed me. I felt you above all others needed to find your own way. It was often painful not to reach out a hand. But even when you were given the choice to run rather than face a Devoured of chaos, you did not take it." Master Rufus inclined his head. "I think of all my students, I have been the proudest of you."

Hmph, said Aaron.

"I will be there for you tomorrow," Rufus went on. "Whatever happens, I will be by your side and Tamara's. I could ask for no greater honor."

Call cleared his throat. "Thanks, Rufus."

Rufus nodded and departed the way he always did, without ceremony. Call headed to his room, bone-weary. Havoc, who had been closed in there, leaped all over him in excitement. Call fell on to the bed and tried to sleep.

He didn't think he would, but, exhausted and overwhelmed, he did.

↑ ≈ △ ○ @

When Call woke, he felt better about the world. He still felt scared about his dad, but he was starting to see that being a Devoured of air might not be the worst thing. At least his dad wasn't going to get old and die like other people's fathers. Alastair would outlive Call. And maybe Alastair couldn't make him dinner and take care of him exactly the way he had before, but Alastair wasn't the greatest cook anyway and Call was probably headed to the Collegium. If he didn't die.

That positive attitude didn't last very long, Aaron said.

"You know me," Call said. "It's not easy to be roommates, especially in the same head, but I'm glad you've been with me. I am glad it was you in my head. Whatever happens, you're the best best friend ever."

Not a lot of people would have been okay with me being in here, said Aaron. *And almost no one would have risked what you did to bring me back to life. You always act like you should be grateful to me for being your friend, just because I'm nice and polite and can make people like me. But I am the one who should be grateful, Call. And I am.*

Call grinned. He felt a little bit embarrassed, but overall surprisingly calm as he put on the stuff the Magisterium had given them to wear. He tied up his boots, slid Miri through his belt, and walked out into the common room, only to see Gwenda and Jasper making out on the couch, which was a bit like walking into a field of daisies on a nice spring morning only to be run over by a truck.

Gack! said Aaron.

"My eyes!" Call yelled, slapping a hand over them.

Tamara walked out of her room just in time to see Jasper and Gwenda spring apart.

"What's going on?" she asked, frowning. "I heard shouting."

Jasper's neck was a little flushed. "We were, uh, just resolving some issues between us." Gwenda was looking shyly at the ground. A small smile curved her mouth.

"I did not see that coming," Call said, a bit dazed.

"Are you kidding?" Tamara elbowed him in the side. "It's been coming for forever! What did you think all that flirting in the car was about?!"

"Flirting?" Jasper said.

Now he was annoyed. But Gwenda and Tamara shared a smile.

"Come on," Tamara said. "We're going to eat breakfast and then we're going to battle the Evil Overlord. The *real* Evil Overlord."

They ate quickly. Gwenda and Jasper held hands the whole time and Call kept wondering if he should have pulled Tamara into a kiss or held her hand or done something. It wasn't fair that Jasper seemed ridiculous a lot, but then turned out to know more than Call about relationships and girls and sometimes even magic.

Tamara likes you, Aaron said. *Remember — today, we're optimists.*

"You're always an optimist," Call muttered under his breath.

At that moment, there was a knock on the door and no more time for discussion. Master Rufus was there with Master Milagros and Assemblyman Graves. They had brought magical rope with them.

"We're not going to tie your arms tightly," said Graves. "But we must give the appearance of going along with his commands."

"Tamara," said Master Milagros, "your sister is here and she wants to talk to you."

"Ravan?" asked Tamara.

"She has not yet been summoned. It's Kimiya who wants to talk with you. She's waiting for you outside the gates."

Call suddenly remembered that Alex had wanted Kimiya handed over to them as well, that he thought she was still his girlfriend.

He also remembered the last time they'd seen Kimiya. She'd been throwing her arms around Alex while he gloated and Tamara looked as if she'd been kicked in the stomach, so Call wasn't inclined to like her much.

Tamara swallowed hard. "Okay. I want to see her."

They headed down the corridor after Master Rufus. Call's optimistic mood was turning quickly into tension as they passed knots of staring, silent students. He was pretty sure most of them didn't know what was going on, but they knew enough to understand that bad things were happening. After all, many of them had seen Alex attack, and they'd all seen the golden tower rising on the horizon like a knife pointing at the sky.

Call kept looking at things as they passed. The door to his old rooms, the ones he'd shared with Tamara and Aaron. The way to the Refectory. The twisting path to the library. The glowing patterns of stones in the walls. The stairs that led to the Gallery. He couldn't stop wondering if it was the last time he'd ever see any of them again.

Suddenly there was a loud bark. Havoc had burst through the door of their rooms and was charging up the hallway. He almost careened into Call, jumping up to put his paws on Call's chest and whining frantically.

"What's going on?" Call patted Havoc's head. "What's wrong, boy?"

Nothing, Aaron said. *He wants to go with you*

"He just wants to come," said Tamara. "We shouldn't leave him behind."

"But he's not a Chaos-ridden wolf anymore," said Call. "It's not fair to bring him."

"Isn't it better," said Rufus, "that he wishes to go with you out of love and loyalty, and not because he is bound to you by chaos? He is your wolf, and I think he has earned his place at your side."

So they headed out of the Mission Gate as a group of six: Master Rufus, Tamara, Gwenda, Jasper, and Call, with Havoc bringing up the rear.

Call saw Kimiya immediately. She was standing with Mr. and Mrs. Rajavi, who were huddled together in a tight family group. All of them were staring warily at Alastair, who hovered translucently near — but not too near — a number of Assembly members.

Given what had happened to Ravan, Call felt like he couldn't blame the Rajavis for looking at Alastair like that. Devoured of any kind must horrify them. But he blamed them anyway.

Tamara immediately detached from their group and ran toward her family, while Call and the others headed toward Alastair and the mages. Havoc and Call greeted Alastair, who brushed an airy hand over Call's hair, stirring the strands without quite touching him. Havoc nosed around Alastair and barked worriedly as he passed through Alastair's legs.

Around them a few other members of the Assembly milled, consulting with some other mages Call didn't know who were explaining about the tower. They had apparently really built the whole thing, with a TV room and a lot of bedrooms, but they'd used the same enchanted materials that they used on the Panopticon. It would be a lot harder for Alex to summon chaos creatures once he was inside — and they planned on sealing up the way in and out once Call and his people were inside.

It would also allow the mages to see through the materials, to watch what happened and come to Call's aid if it was at all possible.

"Although that opens up the danger of Alex Strike being able to summon more elementals of chaos," Graves said.

Tell him you won't need help, Aaron said. *People like to hear that kind of thing.*

But what if we do need help? Call wanted to know.

Just say it, said Aaron. *He's no more or less likely to help no matter what you tell him. But he'll think you're brave and he'll like you better.*

Sometimes Aaron could be a little scary. No, a lot scary.

"I can handle Alex," Call said. Graves did look relieved.

Before he'd have to promise anything else, Call headed toward where Tamara was greeting her family.

"I've been telling everyone how sorry I am," Kimiya said. "I didn't realize how angry Alex was. I thought it would be kind of fun to make our own organization, to have our own thing. Alex said that the Assembly had lied to everyone, that Constantine had been dead for a long time and they just wanted everyone to be afraid. And when I realized it was true — Constantine *had* been gone — I believed all the other stuff he said, too. I never thought he'd hurt Aaron. If I'd known that . . . *everything* would have been different."

Tamara looked at her sister with suspicion. "He wanted to hurt people. He did hurt people."

"I took a chance on someone I cared about," Kimiya said with a pointed look at Call. Which was totally unfair. Well, it was a little unfair. "And I was wrong. But now I'm here to help take him down."

Tamara looked at her sister without warmth or trust. Sometimes Call forgot how unflinchingly stubborn she could be.

"You're not going to be restrained," she told her sister. "You're going to have to be the one who acts first. Once we're inside, you're going to have to make sure the Devoureds have what they need to manifest. Including Ravan."

There was a soft explosion at the sound of Ravan's name. Ravan appeared, a feathery plume of smoke and flame.

"Ravan," Tamara said, and sighed in relief. "You're here."

The Devoured of fire burned her way closer. You could see the shape of Ravan now, her long hair and young face, shaped out of flames. She spoke. "My little family, made of wax and tinder. Do you fear me?"

Mrs. Rajavi shook her head. "I can't look." She turned away, her face tearstained.

"Mother, do you not see me?" Ravan said, flickering. "Will you say you do not know me?"

"Ravan," Mrs. Rajavi said, an immense sadness in her voice, "we knew you before, but we are not sure we know you now."

"Perhaps I am unknowable." Ravan flickered once. "But I will burn for your sake all the same."

"My daughters." Mrs. Rajavi began to sob. "Oh, Ravan. Oh, Tamara and Kimiya, am I going to lose you all? How could this happen? Why our family?"

Tamara and Kimiya came forward to comfort their mother. Call had always had mixed feelings about the Rajavis. They had been cold to him, though kind to Aaron, and they struck him as stern and cruel. But the realization that they were facing losing *all* their children today made Call back away to give them space.

He was immediately buttonholed by Master Rufus. "Call," he said. "It's time to summon the last two Devoured."

Call followed Master Rufus to the center of a loose circle of mages. Jasper and Gwenda were there already. The mages watched in silence as Jasper summoned a small pool of water, which bubbled up around his feet. He knelt down and touched it.

"Lucas," he said, and jumped backward in surprise as the pool shot upward in a column, forming into the shape of Lucas,

Devoured of water. The mages gasped and several of them backed away.

It was Call's turn. He took Greta's geode out of his pocket, bent down, and brought it down with as much force as he could muster against the side of a rock.

It smashed apart into glittering fragments. They all stared at the fragments expectantly. Nothing happened.

"Is it working?" Jasper hissed into Call's ear.

"Yoo-hoo," said a bored voice, and they all turned to see Greta, a rumbling pile of rocks, hovering around the edge of the circle. "I'm here."

She and Lucas waved at each other. Alastair walked over to them slowly, and Ravan drifted along, trailing sparks. The mages all moved away to give the Devoured space, or perhaps to give themselves space from the Devoured.

Hearing shouting, Call turned to find Gwenda in the middle of a fierce argument with Master Rufus. "But I *should* go," she said. "I'm part of the apprentice group! I helped collect the Devoured!"

Master Rufus shook his head. "Absolutely not, Gwenda. Call, Jasper, and Tamara are going because Alex demanded they go. I will not sacrifice the safety of another student for no good reason!"

"It *is* a good reason," Gwenda said. "I can help protect them!" She whirled around and saw Call. "Call, tell him I should go with you."

Call hesitated. "Gwenda, you've been a really good friend, and you've saved our butts a bunch of times since Gold Year started. I'm sorry if I ever underestimated you. But there's no way Alex would let you come with us. The minute he saw someone he didn't ask for, he'd unleash chaos."

Gwenda's eyes glittered angrily, but Call could tell she knew he wasn't lying.

"I don't want to be left behind," she said.

Call looked at Master Rufus. "Can't she come in with the teachers and the Assembly?" he asked. "It would only be fair."

Master Rufus sighed. "I'll see what I can do."

"Everyone, listen!" It was Assemblyman Graves's voice, amplified and echoing. "Callum Hunt. Tamara Rajavi. Jasper deWinter. Please come to stand before me."

Tamara moved reluctantly away from her family. Jasper peeled himself away from Lucas, and a few seconds later they were all standing in front of Assemblyman Graves, along with Havoc, who'd snuck in next to Call.

"That Chaos-ridden wolf —" Graves began angrily.

"He's not Chaos-ridden," said Call. "He's a regular wolf."

Graves stared at Havoc, who blinked normal, wide, greenish wolf eyes at him. "I could have sworn —"

Tamara giggled, and immediately stifled the sound. Graves glared. "Bind their hands," he said.

Master Milagros and Master North came up behind them. Call and the others put their hands behind their backs, and the teachers began to wind strips of flexible enchanted metal around their wrists. Call knew it was necessary, but anger was still boiling inside him.

"These will come off when you tug against them three times in rapid succession," Graves told them. "But they will also be destroyed, so please don't test that in advance."

Tamara looked over at him guiltily, clearly having been just about to do that.

Alastair whirled into the air, becoming only wind, whooshing around Call's head. "I'll be with you," he promised. A moment later, a metal whistle dropped into Call's bound hands. He closed his fingers tightly over it. When he looked at Jasper, a bottle of water was tucked into his pocket. Tamara had an acorn, and Kimiya, a pack of matches that looked scorched on one end, as though Ravan hadn't wanted to stop burning.

"Prepare yourself," said Graves. "We will be flying to the tower."

All around, the mages rose up into the air. Call could feel himself being lifted up, could feel the wind whooshing beneath him, but with Alastair so close, even though his magic was bound, he couldn't be afraid. He remembered how much he had wished for weightlessness, had wanted to fly so that he could avoid all the difficulties of having a leg that hurt a lot.

But that had been a kid's wish. His problems now couldn't be solved by a little magic.

Maybe they can be solved by a lot *of magic*, Aaron said in his head.

They flew over fields and gray highways snaking by underfoot, the forest and the Magisterium retreating behind them. Call glanced over to see Havoc being whirled through the air, his paws flailing, and Tamara nearby, her dark hair flying like a banner. She looked over at him and gave an encouraging smile.

In the distance, the golden tower rose, ever closer. For being built so quickly and for no real purpose but to stall Alex, the shimmering tower was both beautiful and formidable. Call wondered what purpose it might serve after today.

Assuming, of course, that purpose wasn't as his tomb.

They landed on a stretch of grass in front of the single door to the tower. As soon as their feet touched the ground, a dark cloud passed over the sky, signaling Alex's arrival with a bolt of lightning that struck a bare stretch of foliage, blackening it and making everyone jump.

"That ridiculous *child*," Graves ground out.

From the sky, Alex and his retinue heaved into view.

Alex was still on the back of his dragon-shaped chaos elemental but now his outfit had gotten even more elaborate. He wore black — of course — and huge black boots with massive silver buckles in the shape of lightning bolts. Around his shoulders was a cape.

Is that an actual cape? Aaron demanded.

Yep, Call thought. It definitely was — it was even fluttering in the breeze. Alex's hair was spiked up with gel. Flying beside him were two more chaos elementals, both in horselike shapes that looked far less fixed. They sometimes seemed to have wings; other times instead of legs, they seemed to have the long, searching tentacles of octopi. Call guessed one was for Anastasia. The other, he feared, was for Kimiya.

As Alex landed, his cape whipped through the air and Call spotted the dull metal crown on his head, its spikes like teeth. For a moment, even though Call knew it was all calculated, that Alex only cared about the illusion, the illusion worked. Call actually felt a thin tendril of fear and shuddered.

"Assemblypeople of the mage world and other luminaries, I am glad that you've decided to cave to my demands and acknowledge my superiority," said Alex. "This tower you've built me is pretty nice. I plan to reign from it quietly and not disturb you too much. I don't want to do any gross Enemy of Death stuff, like reanimating people or animals. That's not my thing. My thing is letting everyone know how awesome and scary I am."

"You mean everyone in the mage world?" asked Graves. Even though this was for show, he looked furious. "You still intend to keep the great secrets of magic, don't you?"

Alex chortled, and the crowd of creatures around him hooted and cackled. It was much more frightening than anything he'd said. He might be a ridiculous child, as Graves had said, but he had access to enormous power and creatures that could wield it.

"The what?" he sneered.

"The silence of the mage world!" Graves thundered. "We do not tell those without magic of the existence of magic. It endangers them and endangers us. It was difficult enough to build this stupid tower without alerting them to the magic that was happening — "

"My tower isn't stupid," said Alex, and made a casual gesture in Graves's direction. Black fire shot from his fingers and swallowed up the Assemblyman. In seconds, nothing was left but a charred circle in the grass.

Kimiya screamed, then bit the noise back with an obvious effort as Alex frowned at her. The mages were crying out as well, voices echoing around the clearing. Jasper was looking over at Gwenda, his face creased with concern. Tamara just shook her head, looking grim.

Master Rufus stepped forward, into the blackened circle. "Alex Strike," he said.

Alex laughed. "Master Rufus," he said. "Joseph used to talk about you all the time. The great mage who'd taught Constantine Madden. But being your assistant didn't reveal any greatness. Constantine was something in spite of you, not because of you." He flicked his eyes in Call's direction, his mouth stretching into a grin. "After all, look how badly you've done with Callum."

"You may do to me as you did to Graves," said Rufus, and Call tensed. He didn't think he could stand it if Alex wiped his teacher off the face of the world. He'd have to break free of his manacles and that would ruin everything. "But then you will get nothing you want. It will be war with the mage community — and as you've said, you don't want that. You want to be left alone."

"True," said Alex, examining his nails.

"It would be easier for you as well if the ordinary world didn't know about mages," said Rufus. "Think of what you could do. You could use your magic to trick them and make millions."

Alex laughed. "Maybe you *are* brilliant, Rufus. All right. I'll keep the magic to myself." He turned his glimmering, star-filled eyes on Kimiya. "Come along, darling. Don't you still love me?"

Kimiya smiled brilliantly. Call felt uneasy as she ran across the grass toward Alex and hugged his arm. Either she was giving a bravura performance or she was going to betray them all.

Alex leaned down to kiss her. Tamara made a revolted noise. Thankfully it was a short kiss, and Alex broke away grinning, his arm slung over Kimiya's shoulders.

"Have the hostages step forward," Alex said. "Have them walk toward the tower entrance."

Call looked over at Tamara. Her gaze found his. At least they were in this together. Aaron, too. The three of them against the world. Who'd known that when Rufus had picked them, they would become the most important people in Call's life? He looked over at Jasper, at his determined face. Call had never thought they would be friends at all, but somehow whenever his life had needed saving, Jasper had been there holding out a hand — usually with a sarcastic quip, but still there.

He took a step forward, and the others did the same. They moved across the grass onto the ground where it turned into gravel. It was still churned up from the feet of the mages who'd worked on building the tower. Havoc ran to his side, keeping his furred body protectively tight against Call's leg.

Call turned to look back over his shoulder. The mages of the Assembly seemed very far away. He could just see Gwenda, and Rufus —

With a flick of his wrist, Alex sent a blaze of chaos fire toward them all. Call bit back a yell as he realized Alex wasn't attacking. He was throwing up a blockade. The fire rose in an endless wall that curved around them, cutting off Jasper, Call, Tamara, Kimiya, Havoc, and Alex from the mages, but allowing them access to the tower.

Alex sneered. "Let's go see our new home. Callum, you can lead the way."

With a last look at the fire separating him from Master Rufus, Call shuffled toward the door of the tower, a heavy wooden thing. He couldn't open it, so he just stood there until one of the chaos elementals walked over. It snaked out a tentacle toward the door, but where it touched, there was just a hole where the knob had been.

"Automotones!" Alex shouted. "You do it."

The massive metal elemental loomed up out of the smoke that surrounded them and advanced on the door.

Call stared — they'd all fought Automotones once and nearly been killed.

Automotones lurched up to the front doors, his eyes, which were gears, whirring and spinning. His hand shot out, and a vibrating, buzzing blade appeared at the end of it. He sawed at the door until a large chunk of it fell open, crashing onto the ground.

Alex is going to have to get that door fixed, Call thought. *Definitely not a long-term-planning kind of guy.*

Automotones stepped back and they all headed inside with varying degrees of reluctance. The first floor was a large round room, entirely empty except for a rug and a spiral staircase winding upward.

Call went up, and the others followed.

The second floor was all one huge room with massive windows through which Call could see the tops of trees. There were multiple couches and a small kitchen, along with a large screen like the one in the Gallery, where Alex used to project movies. Since Call wasn't sure where Alex wanted him to go, he stopped there, walking toward the far corner. Tamara followed him, then Jasper.

"Now," Call said to them. He pulled three times on his cuffs and his hands were free. Then he brought the whistle to his mouth and blew. No sound came out, only a wild wind that raced around the room to coalesce as Alastair and then to disappear again. Beside him, Lucas manifested — and then Greta. But both of them were gone by the time Alex walked into the room. Call had his hands behind his back, even though they were no longer bound. Tamara and Jasper did the same.

Alex smiled in a smug way, walking around to admire his new digs, billowing cloak swishing around behind him. He was holding one of Kimiya's hands. Call thought the smile on her face seemed forced.

He hoped it was forced.

"Pretty nice here, isn't it?" Alex said, waving an arm around to indicate the whole space — the marble floor, the big couches with their cushions, the enormous TV. "Mom! I'm home!"

Anastasia, Aaron thought. *Of course she's somewhere in here.*

"Alex?" They all stood still as Anastasia came wafting down the staircase from above. She wore a white dress and a sort of gossamer white overcloak. Her icy hair was bound up in a tight knot.

She looked at Call for a long, steady moment. He couldn't read her expression. He felt chilled inside — what if she'd seen what had happened to Graves out the window? What if she was reconsidering everything?

Calm down, Aaron said. *You don't know that.*

But he sounded scared, too.

Anastasia crossed the room to stand near Alex, who beamed. He looked over at Call, wearing a sneer that seemed exaggerated in a practiced-in-the-mirror kind of way.

"You really thought the Magisterium valued your lives enough to save you, didn't you, Call Hunt?" He laughed. "But they handed the three of you right over. They're cowards, just like all the mages. I read all those books in Master Joseph's house, and what I thought when I read them was how weak we'd become. Mages used to be something. They used to use their power for something other than keeping people safe from elementals. Soon you're going to be dead, Callum. And then everyone will have to acknowledge that I'm the greatest mage of any generation, the one who defeated the Enemy of Death."

"You didn't defeat me," Call said. "The Magisterium tied me up, not you."

"No one cares about technical details!" Alex yelled. "No one cares about the real story. Do you think people cared about the fact that Constantine loved his brother or that his mother loved him? No, because that's boring. And they won't care how easy the Magisterium made it to kill you either. They will just care that I did it."

"But not Tamara, right?" Kimiya said. "She's my sister."

Alex hesitated. "She's loyal to my enemy, Kimiya."

"Perhaps we kill the two boys and lock the girl in the dungeon," said Anastasia soothingly.

"This place has a dungeon?" said Jasper.

"Of course it has a dungeon," snapped Alex. "And don't speak unless I speak to you, deWinter. You *should* have been loyal to me. Your father was loyal to Master Joseph."

"My father was wrong," Jasper said quietly. Call stared. He didn't think he'd ever heard Jasper say that before.

"I told you not to speak!" Alex yelled.

"Or you're going to do what?" said Jasper. "Kill me?"

"Enough," said Call. "Maybe nobody has to die. Maybe we could make some sort of deal."

"No deals, Hunt," Alex said. "This time you don't have anything I want. I don't care about bringing people back from the dead. I care about power. And I care about revenge." He grinned. "I want you to line up in front of me," he said, and the black stars in his eyes were glowing like pinpricks. "First Tamara. Then Jasper. Then you, Call. I'm going to kill you in that order, and you're going to watch your friends die, Makar."

"You said you wouldn't hurt Tamara!" Kimiya shrieked.

"I changed my mind," said Alex, raising his hand. It was shimmering with dark light, a halo of blackness around his fingers.

Kimiya darted away from him, reaching for the matchbook with shaking hands.

Alex whirled toward her, smoke wreathing his hands. Call turned to look at Tamara and Jasper, both of them pale, but they shook their heads at him as if to say, *Not quite yet*.

"Just what are you doing?" Alex demanded of Kimiya.

"I was just . . ." Kimiya said, but then her words seemed to run out. She backed away from Alex's approach, clearly terrified. The matchbook dropped out of her hands.

"You're really going to betray me?" Alex demanded. "Me? Who was going to save you from your boring old life?"

"This isn't what you said it would be like," Kimiya said. "You never told me you were going to hurt people."

"So you conspired against me? With these losers?" Alex shook his head. He lifted his hand, and a bolt of chaos grew from his palm; Tamara flew at him, abandoning the pretense of having bound hands. He swung his arm with the strength of chaos, flinging her aside, and Call's hands flew apart, too, rage filling him — how dare Alex touch Tamara? How dare he threaten his friends?

He was still summoning chaos inside himself when Alex let fly a bolt of black fire. It shot straight at Kimiya

Chaos exploded from Call's hand at the same moment. The two forks of dark lightning met in the air. Neither dissolved, though. They slammed into each other and ricocheted into the wall of the tower, blowing the stone to powder.

"Whoa," said Jasper. Call agreed. The chaos had smashed through rock, metal, and glass, and now there was a truck-size hole in the wall of the tower. On the other side of the hole, Call could see the field in front of the tower. The wall of chaos fire was dying down, though it looked like the mages still couldn't cross it. A lot of them were gaping up at the tower, though, a few pointing and gasping.

Then Automotones's massive metal face filled the space. Kimiya screamed. Tamara reached for her sister and yanked her down onto the ground. The acorn skittered from her hand. Jasper knocked the bottle of water out of his pocket and it hit the floor, leaking water everywhere. Call pulled the whistle from his pocket, gripping it tightly in his hand.

Anastasia leaned down and seized the matchbook.

Alex turned toward Call, his smirk plastered back on. "Oh, so you thought you were going to fight me! That's why you came here willingly. The Magisterium and the Assembly are going to pay for setting me up, but you're going to pay first."

"Am I?" said Call.

"I am chaos!" Alex shouted. "I have become the void!"

"Oh, shut up," said Call. "No one's interested."

Alex gaped at him. Call couldn't help it. He'd started to grin. Because behind Alex, Alastair was swirling into being, air coalescing to form his towering shape. Havoc barked as Lucas rose out of the puddle on the floor, shimmering and silver. And from Tamara's smashed acorn, Greta emerged, a river of dirt and earth reaching upward.

"What is this?" Alex whirled around, raising his hand again. He stared in disbelief. "They're *Devoured*. But why are they here? *Why are you here?*"

"Anastasia," Call called. "Strike a match!"

Her pale eyes turned to him, her expression strange.

Mom. You were supposed to say "Mom," Aaron reminded him, but it was too late. Call hadn't and now she knew he'd been lying to her.

Everything was going wrong.

Anastasia took a step toward Call, her eyes flashing. A gray blur flew between them — it was Havoc, who clamped his jaws down on Anastasia's wrist. She screamed and dropped the matches. Alex sent another bolt of chaos flying at Havoc, but the wolf leaped out of the way and the black fire smashed into the wall of the tower. More stone crumbled.

"You're making me ruin my tower!" Alex shouted at Call. "You always ruin everything!"

Call couldn't deny it. More than being a Makar, that was pretty much his superpower.

Kimiya had the matches again. In shaking hands, she pulled one out and struck it. It caught alight and then Ravan was there, flaring to life.

She looked at her sisters and a wicked smile grew on her face.

"Get ready," Call said, under his breath.

Ready, said Aaron.

"What are you doing?" Alex shouted as the Devoured rushed toward him.

It was like the world was collapsing in on itself. Every element colliding with chaos — the force of air, the burning heat of fire, the relentlessness of water, the powerful weight of earth. They fell on Alex with the destructive power of a thousand tornadoes ripping across fields, a thousand volcanoes erupting with a force that blackened the sky, a thousand earthquakes buckling and tearing cities apart, and a thousand floods carrying away whole towns in a froth of churning, tearing water. They were human, but not human; Call shielded his face with his hand as they savagely tore the chaos that surrounded Alex, as they were ripping off bits with their hands, oily patches of nothingness that dissolved entirely in the air.

Alex howled a great shriek of agony that sent a bolt of fear through Call. What if they killed him? What if they destroyed his body?

That wasn't the plan.

Automotones reared back his head and bellowed, then snapped his jaws toward Jasper. Jasper spun on his heel and flung fire at Automotones, blast after blast of flame that sent the metal monster reeling backward, his plates and gears glowing red with heat.

Good to see Jasper finally got the hang of fire, said Aaron.

Automotones staggered toward them again. The black fire of chaos had died down outside, and the mages were rushing at the tower, slamming at the closed doors below. The tower shook.

Alex was still screaming. He tipped his head back with a howl and darkness erupted from his eyes — two long trails of blackness that shot up into the air. Kimiya was screaming her head off. Tamara was on her feet, making a shield of air to protect her.

Alex turned his head to the side. He was surrounded by the Devoured on all sides. Black tears leaked from his eyes. He held out a hand. "Mother," he croaked. *"Mother."*

Anastasia staggered back from him, her face a mask of horror. Alex's face worked, and one last bolt of chaos shot from his hand. It was weak — Call could feel its weakness — but strong enough. It hit Anastasia in the chest, lifting her off her feet and dropping her to the ground, a black hole seared across the front of her chest.

Alex went limp.

Now, said Aaron.

Call called on everything he'd ever learned about the soul tap and sent his concentration spinning toward Alex. He could *see* Alex's soul, the glow and light of it, no longer blackened with chaos. He felt it, almost as though he held it in his hands, pulsing and sparking, wrapped around with cords of hate, ambition, and pain. Call could see the kid who had liked being popular, who liked being Master Rufus's assistant, but who never felt like it was enough. He saw the kid who had crafted elaborate illusions out of movies, weaving in his friends and himself, always himself — as the winner, the victor, the person who got everything in the end. Call saw the part of Alex that had felt bereft when his father died, abandoned to a woman with her own agenda, her own obsession. He saw his ambition grow and bloom and twist. Saw his hatred of Call, his resentment, his desire to be the winner. Call saw all of that, saw Alex's soul, whole and human and flawed.

With all his strength, Call braced himself — and tried to push it out of Alex's body.

He felt a terrible echo in the deed. The body he lived in was stolen, and now he was stealing another. But even weak, Alex was a Makar and he fought back. He pushed, too, straining against Call's consciousness, forcing Call's physical body to his knees.

You will never defeat me, Alex's voice declared, echoing in Call's head. For a moment, Call felt uprooted, adrift. What if because he wasn't born into his body, it was harder to stay in? What if he couldn't hold on, even as Aaron left him behind? Panic started to bloom in his chest. The weight of Alex pushing back shoved him flat against the ground, his elbows braced, shoulders straining.

I can't do this, he thought. *I can't.*

Maybe one of us couldn't, but both of us will, came Aaron's voice, sure and strong. He joined his thoughts to Call's and together they surged back at Alex, thrusting him loose from the bright lines that moored his soul to his body, pushing him out. Pushing him out into nothing.

The cords that bound Alex's soul to his body frayed and snapped and he was gone, without even a scream or a cry. Call didn't know where souls went — he guessed that no one did — but he was sure it was someplace far beyond the void.

Aaron, Call thought. *Aaron, you have to go.*

It was as if he could feel Aaron's soul taking a shaking, hesitant breath. Call reached for Aaron one last time — for his counterweight, for the soul that was the most familiar in the world to him. It was as if his hands were brushing over Aaron's soul, holding it for a moment, and letting it free.

Alex's body jerked once, and he took a gasping breath.

Aaron, Call thought. *Did it work?*

But there was no response. There was only an echoing silence in Call's ears. He was alone. He hadn't realized how unused to being truly alone in his own head he was.

Sound smashed in as Call realized the battle had been raging on. The chaos dragon had eaten away another section of the tower. Dozens of mages had flown up to the tower's second level, helped by Alastair and the power of air, and were joining Jasper and Tamara in battling Automotones. Greta, Lucas, and Ravan had also joined in — Greta was hurling rocks at the chaos elementals, Lucas was directing streams of superheated water at them, and Ravan was shooting bolts of fire.

Inside the tower, Kimiya had Anastasia cradled in her lap and seemed to be trying to keep her from dying.

Call staggered to his feet. "A-Alex?"

Alex opened his eyes. Kimiya gasped: They had returned to being blue, no longer black and star-silvered. Coughing violently and looking dazed, Alex pushed himself up onto his knees.

The gestures seemed familiar. He wasn't moving like Alex did. He was moving like Aaron. He had his gestures. Call's heart leaped into his throat. Was he imagining it, or had their plan actually worked?

Master Rufus came racing up the stairs and burst into the room; after him came Master North and Master Milagros. They stared at the scene in front of them — Anastasia dying, the Devoured still hovering in the room, the huge chunks torn from the walls.

And Alex, in the middle of it all.

"Alex!" Call cried. "Alex, stop the chaos creatures. Show them you're on our side now."

"Stop," Alex shouted, in a voice that was both like his usual voice and different. "Stop, chaos creatures! I *command* you to stop."

The dragon abruptly paused its movements. Automotones roared. From outside the tower there were more echoing sounds as the chaos creatures heard him.

"Go back to chaos!" Alex cried. "Return to the place you came from!"

More Masters were crowding up behind North, Rufus, and Milagros. They all stared at Alex, who stood with his hands flung out, ordering the chaos creatures to disperse.

"They're going," said Milagros in amazement. "Look!"

Through the smashed hole in the wall, Call could see the chaos creatures turn and retreat, Automotones leading the way. As they went, they seemed to shimmer and vanish, each one disappearing, leaving only smudges of darkness hanging like smoke against the sky.

The mages of the Magisterium were cheering. Ravan, Lucas, Greta, and Alastair had disappeared, probably worried that they wouldn't be particularly welcome now that the immediate danger was over.

"Call. Come here." It was Kimiya, gesturing him over urgently. Tamara was kneeling down beside her, summoning earth magic to heal Anastasia.

Call didn't move to stop her. Nothing was going to help

Anastasia now. She smiled at him, and there was blood on her teeth. "Con," she whispered.

Tamara bit her lip, color flaring in her cheeks. She'd always hated it when Anastasia called Callum by Constantine Madden's name.

"Con," Anastasia said again. "I know what you did. I know."

He reached out and took her hand, because he had never meant for her to be hurt. He'd never meant for anyone to be hurt.

"I'm sorry," he told her. "Really, really sorry."

"Sometimes, you're nothing like my son was, nothing at all," she said, then raised her voice. "Mages of the Magisterium, I have a final confession!"

Alex had sunk back down onto his heels.

"It was I who controlled Alex," said Anastasia, and the whole room of mages stood breathless and silent, listening. "It was I who controlled everything — not Master Joseph, not Constantine Madden, me. They were all my pawns. You were all my pawns."

"How?" demanded Master North. "How did you do it?"

"I learned from the best," she said. "My son Constantine, the Enemy of Death. He kept Jericho in his thrall for years, forcing him to be his counterweight and give up pieces of his soul. When Alex first became my stepson, I began to control him. At first it was small things. Later I made him totally obedient to Master Joseph. He had no choice but to obey his commands." She coughed, and blood sprayed across her white clothes. "Do what you like with him. I don't care. I never loved him."

"Then why are you telling us this?" Master Rufus demanded.

"I want the credit," Anastasia croaked. "It was I who made him a Devoured, I who caused this tower to be built. The Magisterium took my son from me but in the end it served me and my desires." She looked at Call. He forced himself to smile at her, and something in her face relaxed. "You can hurt me no more," she said in a whisper, and her eyes fell closed, her head lolling to the side.

Tamara cried out. Gwenda had run across the room to Jasper, and he was holding her, looking grim.

Alex was looking at her, his face ashen. "What have I done?" he asked, which seemed like a perfectly appropriate question and one also wrenched from a place deep inside of him. Alex turned his gaze on the mages, on Master Rufus. "You should arrest me. Someone should arrest me."

"Wait!" Call said. "You heard Anastasia. She forced him to do all those things. She forced him to become a Devoured of chaos. You agreed to forgive him."

"We agreed to interview him," Master North said. "Graves agreed to it, anyway. And thanks to him, Graves is dead."

Alex hung his head. *Aaron*, Call thought. *Aaron, look at me.*

But he didn't. And Call didn't know whether to think of him as Alex or Aaron, didn't know if Aaron's soul was intact inside Alex's body, or if Aaron was in agony, crushed by guilt or horror or a million different other things. Or maybe his soul had been shredded — maybe he was no one now, neither Alex nor Aaron.

And then Call noticed Havoc. Havoc had crept to Alex's side and was nosing gently at his hand, the way he'd once done to Aaron. And absently, Alex — Aaron, it had to be Aaron — reached down and stroked the wolf's head.

Call saw Master Rufus staring at the wolf, his eyes narrowed. Before he could say anything, Mr. and Mrs. Rajavi flew up the stairs, racing into the room to embrace Tamara and Kimiya. "You did it, my darlings," said Mrs. Rajavi, kissing them both. "You're heroes. I'm so proud of you."

Privately, Call thought Tamara deserved all the credit and Kimiya none, but he kept it to himself.

Alastair appeared in a whirl of air, startling everyone. "The others are gone," he said. "It seems this is finally over."

"As soon as they let Alex go," Call insisted, and his father gave him a very confused look.

Aaron — because Call was sure Alex was Aaron, absolutely sure, except that he really wished that Aaron would say something to confirm it — didn't speak at all.

"Enough," said Master Rufus. "Let's leave this tower. It can harm no one to restrain . . . Alex. We will keep his hands bound until he has stood trial before the Assembly."

"We will take Anastasia's body to the Collegium to prepare it for burial," said Master Cameron, one of the mages Call recognized from his brief visit to the Collegium during his Bronze Year.

Rufus nodded. It was clear everyone was now looking to him as they once had to Graves. "Once we're sure no one else is badly hurt, we can proceed to deciding what we're going to do with Alex."

"How come you're acting as though you're in charge?" Master North, who didn't seem to have gotten the memo, demanded.

"I've been asked to join the Assembly and I've agreed. For a long time, I wanted to stay distant from the mage world. It's not easy to be best known for teaching one of our great enemies. But this time I've said yes." Master Rufus looked grave. "Now can we get these students to safety? They've risked enough for us."

Call tried to say something to Aaron, but Master North was already levitating him in the air. Tamara reached out her hand to Aaron as well, but he went by without reacting. Call's and Tamara's eyes met, the same question in both of them.

Was Aaron in there — and if he was, was he okay?

CHAPTER SIXTEEN

THE TRIP BACK to the Magisterium was a blur. Call found himself hurried into the infirmary, then wrapped in blankets by Master Amaranth. Tamara and Jasper were enfolded in their own blankets beside him. The news came that Anastasia had been pronounced dead, which Call had already known. Still, the words felt stark.

Gwenda came in and hugged them all. She brought Rafe and Kai with her and they hugged Jasper a lot and high-fived Tamara and Call. They reported that the school was celebrating and everyone was acting like they'd never been suspicious of Call at all. Since Kai and Rafe were also acting like they themselves had never been suspicious of Call, he could believe it.

Alastair came in to say that he, Greta, Lucas, and Ravan were getting out of the Magisterium before they wound up locked up with Alex. He'd had Master Rufus's promise that some kind of better system for dealing with the Devoured was going to be worked out at the upcoming meeting, but until then they were going to make themselves scarce.

"I'll see you once you've graduated," Alastair promised Call. "Don't worry about me, either. I need to get back home and make sure the house and all my things are dealt with properly."

They paused awkwardly for a moment. Alastair reached down to touch Call's cheek. It felt like a brush of air. "I'm so sorry," Call blurted. "Because of me, this happened. Because of me, you're a Devoured of air, and you'll never fix up cars again or go to the movies —"

"I'll go to the movies," Alastair said gently. "I'll drift around in the back. I won't have to pay to get in!"

"You know what I mean," said Call.

"Listen, Call. All my life I wished I'd been able to do more. More to defeat the Enemy of Death. More to avenge Sarah. And I've realized now, that feeling is gone, like I've finally been able to put it to bed. I've finally been able to do enough."

"By destroying Alex?" Call said.

"By raising you," said Alastair. "You're a good person, Call, and a fighter. And a heck of a mage." His eyes shone. "I can't tell you how worth it it's all been."

Call felt his heart lift. He almost asked Alastair when they were going to head home together, but Master Amaranth was giving them a sharp look for talking. Alastair winked and disappeared.

Call sighed. "Master Amaranth? I was wondering if I could go rest in my room. I'm not in pain, but I am really tired."

Master Amaranth regarded him suspiciously. He guessed that she had a lot of kids either trying to get in or out of her office. Her snake, coiled like a stole over her shoulders, flashed between sky blue and yellow. "If you really feel you should, Callum. If you feel at all dizzy or faint, come back immediately."

"Can I go with him?" Tamara said, standing up and shrugging off her blanket.

Master Amaranth threw up her hands. "I suppose so. After all, who am I to delay the heroes of the Magisterium with a little thing like making sure they're well?"

Jasper had looked ready to ask to go, too, until Gwenda had come in to the infirmary and hugged all of them. Then, all of a sudden, he'd seemed to develop a pain in his leg that required Gwenda to sit by his bed and tell him how brave he'd been.

Call escaped into the hall, Tamara behind him.

"We're going to see Aaron, right?" she asked.

He nodded. "If we can get down there. We don't have the key anymore."

"Warren led us there once," Tamara said, and proceeded to call to the little lizard. "Waaaaarrrrrren, where are you? The time is actually over. We did it. It's over. But we need your help one last time."

A tongue snapped down from the ceiling, smacking Tamara in the nose and causing her to rub it vigorously. "Gross!" she yelled. "That's disgusting, Warren."

The elemental lizard made a wheezing hiss that might have been laughter. Then he crawled down from the ceiling and with each movement, he got bigger. The gems on his back shone with a fiery light as he grew and grew and grew. By the time he was done, he was larger than Havoc, with a mouth full of gemstone teeth.

"Uh," said Call. "Whoa. I didn't know you could do that. How come I didn't know you could do that?"

"In your past is your future," Warren said. "And in your future, your past."

Call sighed, realizing there was no chance that Warren, no matter his size, was going to give him an honest answer. "Can you take us the secret way to where Aar — I mean *Alex* is being held?"

"Another secret? Yes, Warren will keep another secret. Warren will take you to the place. But you will owe Warren and someday Warren will ask for something, too."

"I thought saving the world was what we did in return," said Tamara tartly.

Ignoring her, Warren set off. It was actually easier to follow the larger version of him. He still was able to climb along the ceiling, which made Call a little nervous. He was afraid he was going to get dropped down on.

They made it through the secret entrance into the elemental prisons, through the chamber of fire and then into the chamber of air, where strange whooshing elementals were enclosed in cages of clear crystal that reminded Call of his time in the Panopticon.

They spotted Aaron easily. He was sitting on the floor of a small cell.

Master Rufus was pacing in front of it. "We're going to the Assembly meeting in a few minutes," he said. "But first, I want you to tell me what's going on."

Aaron looked at the wall. It was shocking how much he looked like Aaron now to Call, and not Alex. As if the shape of his face had subtly changed. Call knew he'd never answer Master Rufus, not when the answer could get Call and Tamara in trouble.

"What do you mean, what's going on?" Call said. "You heard what Anastasia said. Alex was in her thrall before. Now he's free."

Rufus's expressive eyebrows rose. "And just what are you doing here? A place you're absolutely not supposed to be. I am sure there's no mystery to that either."

"Uh," Call said. When Aaron wasn't in his head, it was a lot harder to come up with the kind of answers that teachers liked.

Rufus shook his head. "I don't believe it anyway," he said flatly. "Controlling someone is powerful magic, the kind that requires constant supervision. Yet Anastasia Tarquin rarely visited the Magisterium."

"She was here during our Bronze Year," said Tamara. "That was when Alex started to go evil."

"Even if he were being controlled," said Rufus, "even if her death freed him, he would still be Alex Strike. But Havoc approached him and treated him as if he were one of you. Someone he knew and loved."

In the cage, Aaron shook his head very slightly. Call wished he could still read Aaron's mind and knew what he was trying to communicate.

"When you said you wanted to give Alex a second chance, I wondered what you knew," said Rufus. "I knew you would never forgive Alex for killing Aaron. But you were insistent that he live. And here he is, seemingly unharmed. And seemingly no longer Alex."

Tamara swallowed. "What do you mean?" she whispered.

"I think you know what I mean," said Rufus. "But I want you to say it. Let me make one thing clear: The Assembly meeting that will determine what happens to Alex is about to start. If you tell me nothing, I will oppose his freedom in every way I can. If you tell me the truth now, I *may* help you."

"Those aren't great terms," said Call.

Master Rufus crossed his arms over his chest. "They're the only terms you're going to get."

"Fine," Call said, casting all caution to the winds. "That's not Alex. That's Aaron."

Aaron looked at the ground. Master Rufus didn't seem surprised. "Aaron didn't die on the battlefield."

"His soul went into me," said Call. "I carried him in my head. But we knew he needed a body. And Alex killed Aaron! He *murdered* him, for no reason! It was only fair he should be the one to give Aaron back a body and a life."

"And you knew about this, Tamara?" said Rufus.

Tamara slipped her hand into Call's. Even in the tension of the moment, Call noticed the warmth of her fingers; her touch gave him confidence, and he stood a little straighter. "I knew about all of it," she said. "I agreed to protect Call *and* Aaron. If Aaron hadn't taken over Alex's body, Alex would have kept on fighting until Call was dead — and he would have hurt a lot more people than that. You saw what he did to Graves. Now a good person is alive because of what we did."

"Doling out life and death as if you were small gods," Master Rufus said. "What did I teach you? What is it about my methods that encourages my students to such heights of arrogance?" The last part came out a lot louder than Rufus usually spoke to them, even when they were disappointing him.

Call was taken aback, but it was Aaron who spoke. "It wasn't your fault. Or I guess if it is your fault, then it's because you keep picking Makars."

Rufus gave him a long look. "Go on, Mr. Stewart."

Aaron sighed. "Chaos magic isn't like other kinds. I bet there are lots of kids at the Magisterium who've used their magic for all kinds of weird stuff. Faking precious gems and selling them, enchanting magical things to make non-magic people hop on one foot or whatever, showing people movies with faked endings. That's what testing the limits of regular magic gets you. Testing the limits of chaos magic gets you . . . this."

"You sound like yourself, Aaron," Rufus said. "If I wasn't so angry, I'd be amazed."

"We don't want more trouble," Call said. "I didn't want *any* of this trouble. I didn't even want to come to mage school, if you remember."

Rufus looked like he was about to object, but Call cut him off. "I wasn't right about that — but what I'm trying to say is that we're not going to play with life and death anymore, or anything like that. We're going to the Collegium and we're going to keep our heads down."

"Very well," said Master Rufus. "I will think about what you've said and I will make my decision at the Assembly meeting." He waved a hand and the sheer wall keeping Aaron locked away came down. "Even if you can't tell the whole truth," he advised Aaron, "speak from the heart."

Tamara went over and hugged Aaron tightly. "I'm so glad you're back," she said, and Call felt a tremor of familiar jealousy. He pushed it away, just glad to have his friend back in the world.

Aaron walked over to Call and hugged him just as tightly as he and Tamara had embraced. "Thank you," Aaron said, his voice soft. "For everything. For my life. You're my counterweight, my balance. You always will be."

"Come along," said Master Rufus, guiding Aaron to walk in front of him. With a wave of Rufus's wrists, Aaron was wearing restraints. "Before we're late for the Assembly meeting."

Call and Tamara followed Master Rufus out of the halls of elementals and through a few echoing chambers, until they came to the same large room the Assembly had used before. There was the same table and this time Aaron was placed in the center, so that he stood there, with everyone staring at him. Call remembered what that had felt like.

"Alex Strike," Mrs. Rajavi began, and Call could hear the anger in her voice. "You have murdered one of our members in front of us. You are responsible for many more deaths and much disruption. Yet you claim you were under the influence of Anastasia Tarquin. Do you have any proof of that?"

"She confessed it," said Aaron. "Everything I did was under her influence."

"Do you remember being controlled?" demanded Master North. He was sitting in the place Graves had once sat. "Do you remember what you did?"

Aaron shook his head. "I don't have any memory of being a Devoured of chaos," he said — which, Call figured, was the truth. "Or of betraying the Magisterium. I'm loyal to the

Magisterium, and I hate Master Joseph." He spoke with a venom that would have been hard to fake.

"You understand it isn't easy to believe you," said Master Milagros, but her voice was gentler. "We all saw you burn the woods around the Magisterium. We saw you torture children and murder Master Rockmaple."

"That was Anastasia," Aaron said. He looked more nervous now, probably because he actually *was* lying, which always made him uncomfortable. It hadn't been Anastasia, it had been Alex.

They're both dead, now, Call thought at him as hard as he could. For once, he missed the time he'd been able to speak to Aaron silently. *You're not hurting them. It doesn't matter what anyone thinks about them, it just matters if you're okay.*

"Why did she do all of that?" said Master Rufus. His expression was impossible to read. "Why use you to try to bring down the school, the Assembly?"

"She blamed and hated all mages for the death of her sons," said Aaron. "I thought at first I would be like a new son to her, but I was just something for her to use. She'd learned a little from Constantine's books. She was able to hold a small piece of my soul, to control it, like the Order of Disorder controls the animals in the woods. When everyone found out about Aaron, that's when she acted. She took control of me and made me murder him and take his Makar powers. I don't remember anything after that."

Tamara bumped Call's shoulder with her own. "That was pretty good," she whispered. *Pretty good lying,* she meant.

Murmurs went around the room. "She did confess," Call heard someone say, and "But what if he's not telling the truth? What if they were in on it together?" said someone else.

"I think it is time to put this to a vote," said Master North. "All in favor of accepting Alex Strike's story as true and allowing him back at the Magisterium, raise your hands."

Call knew he and Tamara weren't allowed to vote. Tamara was staring at her parents with mute appeal: after a long moment, both raised their hands. It seemed to Call that a lot of people had raised their hands — but, he saw to his horror, Master Rufus's hand was down. Aaron stared at his Master, pale with shock.

"All right," said Master North, making a note. "Now, everyone in favor of sending Alex Strike to the Panopticon, raise their hands."

Just as many hands went up, now Master Milagros's among them. But Master Rufus still kept his hands flat on the table.

"Rufus?" said North, pausing with pen in hand.

"I abstain," Rufus said in a voice as dry as gravel.

Master North shrugged. "Then it's a tie," he said. "Rufus, you're going to have to vote. We need a tiebreaker."

"He has to," Tamara whispered. "He *has* to vote for — for *him*."

She looked at Aaron. Call was barely able to keep his seat. His fingernails were digging into his palms so hard it hurt.

Master Rufus rose to his feet. "There is one thing that can determine the truth here," he said. "Rather than a vote cast on intuition alone, I would like to see Alexander Strike and Callum Hunt pass through the Fifth Gate."

The room exploded. Master Rufus remained expressionless through it all, like a rock in a churning stream.

"Call is my apprentice," said Rufus. "Alex was my assistant. I can tell you they are both ready. The Fifth Gate, the Gate of Gold, is about doing good works in the world, about genuinely intending to do good. If the gate opens for them and allows them through, then they have learned that lesson. Note that Constantine never walked through that gate; he left the school before he could be asked to do so. If Alex can walk through the Gate of Gold, then I believe we should accept that whatever he's been forced to do by circumstance, he has a pure heart."

The mages quieted down, listening to Rufus speak. When he was done, there was a long silence.

"Very well," said Master North finally. "I would very much like to see these two tested by the gate. In alchemy, gold is considered to be the purest of metals. The Gate of Gold will test the purity of your hearts. Fail, children, and be locked away forever. There will be no more chances. Go back to your rooms, don your uniforms, and prepare yourselves."

"If they're walking through the gate," Tamara said, "I am walking with them."

"And if you fail, you will share their fate?" asked Master North. Master Rufus did not look pleased.

"No," said Mrs. Rajavi, standing. "Of course she won't. No one doubts that Tamara has been acting on the behalf of the

Magisterium and the mage world. Her fate is not in question."

Mr. Rajavi stood with his wife. "Leave our daughter out of this."

"I broke Call out of prison. I believe in Alex," Tamara told the mages. "Enough to share their fate. I am walking through the gate with them. And if the gate rejects me, then I don't deserve anything different from what they get."

"Tamara —" Call started. He believed she'd make it through the gate, but he didn't like even the specter of her and the Panopticon anywhere close together.

"Very well," said Master North, cutting Call off. "You three go and prepare. I will see you in the Hall of Graduates."

Call's whole body was trembling with half-released tension as he made his way back to their rooms in the Magisterium. Tamara held his hand. Aaron was heaving shaky breaths, like he was fighting down a panic attack.

"I think we did it," Call said finally, as they walked into their rooms. "All we have to do is walk through the final gate. We'll have completed the Magisterium and avoided prison."

Aaron nodded slowly, letting out a long sigh and sitting down on the sofa. "Let's just hope this Gate of Gold lets us through. And thank you, both of you, for bringing me back to life. That's a little awkward to say, but it was a lot more awkward to pull off."

Tamara hit him on the shoulder. "Welcome back," she said,

and he folded her into a hug. Both of them smiled and Call was grinning, too.

"How does it feel?" Call asked. "To be all the way back."

Aaron turned to him and even though it was Alex's face, it was easy to see Aaron's spirit shining through. "You mean not rattling around in your noggin? It feels a little weird, like this body is a suit that doesn't quite fit yet. But it's nice and quiet. Living in your head was like living in some kind of maelstrom of self-recrimination, stubbornness, and ridiculous ideas." He turned to Tamara. "Seriously. You should see the ones he doesn't say out loud. He was toying with one way of beating Alex that involved chewing gum, paperclips, and —"

"Okay," Call said, interrupting as he steered Aaron toward Jasper's room, where he hoped there would be an extra uniform. "We better go get ready. Can't keep the mages waiting!"

He and Tamara both headed to their own rooms to change. Havoc was asleep on Call's bed, paws in the air. Call felt a pang — who would take care of Havoc if he didn't make it through the final gate? He rubbed his hand over his wolf's head, trying not to think about anything else, and went to his wardrobe.

A clean deep red Gold Year uniform hung there. Call's previous clothes had been destroyed, covered in mud and blood. At some point their actual graduations had started to become very blurred. This wasn't the first gate they'd walked through at a different time from the rest of their classmates. It would, however, be the last.

He changed and went to get Miri, lying on his night table. He strapped her to his belt. He was ready.

Except not quite. There was a knock on the door and Tamara slipped into his room. She wore her Gold Year uniform, too, her cheeks flushed, her hair coiled up in a braid at the back of her head. Call thought she looked beautiful, and was relieved that for once there was no one in his head to make fun of him. He could just look at Tamara and think about how much he liked her, and even if someday she didn't like him back, even if that someday was now, as long as she was always his friend, it would be okay.

"I came because there was something I wanted to tell you," she said. "Something I couldn't tell you before."

Call was instantly alarmed. "What?"

"This," she said, stepping into his arms and kissing him.

For a second Call was worried he might be too shocked to move, but that turned out not to be a concern. He flung his arms around Tamara and kissed her back, and it felt like flying. She wrapped her arms around his neck and he held her even closer, and the kiss was incredibly soft and sweet and at the same time like having stars and comets explode in his brain.

She drew back just a little, and there were tears in her eyes. "There," she said. "I couldn't do that while Aaron was in your head."

"You mean it?" he said. "Like, you mean that — that you like me? Because I love you, Tamara, and I want to be your boyfriend."

So much for it being okay if she was just his friend, Call thought. He must have been temporarily insane. He stared at her anxiously as her eyes narrowed — oh God, she was going to say no. She was going to say she'd only kissed him for closure, or because she felt sorry for him, or because she assumed he was going to die shortly.

"I love you, too," she said. "And I really hate the idea of anyone else being your girlfriend, so I guess it had better be me."

This time, Call was the one who kissed her, and she went up on her toes to kiss him back. They were still kissing when Havoc started barking, and when they drew apart, giggling, Havoc was scratching at Call's bedroom door.

"Ugh, that means someone's here," Tamara said, drawing away from Call reluctantly. "I guess we'd better go see if it's Master Rufus."

They went out into the living room, holding hands. But it wasn't Master Rufus — it was Gwenda and Jasper. Jasper looked at their linked hands and raised his eyebrows. "Could it be love's young dream?" he inquired.

"Shut up, Jasper." Gwenda hit him lightly on the shoulder.

"Yeah," Call echoed nonsensically. He could make fun of them for kissing, too, but at that moment, he didn't feel like making fun of anyone. He was both too happy and too scared, a strange combination.

"We're supposed to take you to the last gate," Jasper said. "The rest of the mages are waiting. It's so not fair that you get to graduate early and I don't. That's definitely going to make the Collegium more likely to give you a good spot." He sighed. "But — at least my dad's going to be okay."

Call nodded. He couldn't bring himself to feel bad that Jasper's dad was going to stay in prison for helping Master Joseph, but he was glad for Jasper's sake that nothing else would happen to him. "The Collegium is more likely to bar us from it," he said, trying to pep Jasper up. "In case we happen to accidentally burn it to the ground."

"Yeah," said Tamara. "And the choices were 'graduate early' or 'go to prison, do not pass go, do not collect a million dollars.'"

Right then, Aaron stepped out of Jasper's room. Everyone froze. He was wearing a uniform that actually fit him, so Call guessed it wasn't one of Jasper's.

Aaron's smile was hopeful and full of nervousness. "I wasn't . . . myself. Before. But I am now. I hope you can forgive me."

"You're actually on Team Good now?" Jasper asked.

Aaron nodded.

Jasper gave him a long, steady look. "Huh."

"Come on," said Gwenda. "Let's find out if he's on the up-and-up."

Together, they trooped through the caverns of the Magisterium, passing a room with long stalagmites and steaming mud heating the air. They ducked through another doorway and into the Hall of Graduates. An archway Call had never seen before was shimmering with golden light. The carved words *Prima Materia* glowed on the wall above as though illuminated from within their grooves.

A smaller crowd had gathered to witness this. Master Rufus and Master Milagros, Master North and the Rajavis. Gwenda and Jasper murmured last words of luck and good wishes to Call and Tamara before crossing the room to stand with the teachers and Assembly members.

Master Rufus was wearing a tight smile, which relaxed as they came in. "Tamara, Alex, Call. You are ready to pass through the final gate of the Magisterium, the Gate of Balance. Previously, your studies allowed you to walk through control, affinity, creation, and transformation. Long ago, you passed through the First Gate, the Gate of Control, and became a mage in your own right. Now, once you pass through the Gate of Balance, you will be not only a mage but also a member in good standing of the mage world. Passing through the gate demands that you are able to put aside your own desires and emotions for the good of others. If you can see the gate, then you're ready to be tested. Tamara Rajavi, you first."

She stepped forward, shoulders back, and walked up to the gate. As she had with the very first gate she stepped through, she put up her hand to touch it. Then she disappeared from view.

"Now you, Alex Strike."

"Okay," Aaron said, looking nervous. He wiped his hands against his pants. Stepping up to the gate, he took a deep breath, then walked through, disappearing as well.

Call couldn't see either of them. He couldn't see if they'd made it to the other side. All he could see was Master Rufus's implacable expression and the eyes of the other mages, waiting for him to be judged.

"Callum Hunt," said Master Rufus "Your turn."

Call swallowed and moved toward the gate.

"Wait!" a voice called. "Stop!"

Call whirled around. To his surprise, there was Alastair. He looked much as he always had, except a little blurry around the edges, and he was no longer wearing his glasses. He glanced over at Master Rufus, and Call realized his teacher must have summoned his dad to the ceremony.

"We need to do this *now*," called Master North.

Alastair disappeared, and reappeared again only a foot from Call. Call stepped toward his father, and they hugged quickly. Alastair was actually starting to feel substantial — Call could almost feel the texture of his jacket. "I went through the Gate of Balance, once," Alastair murmured. "You can, too. You're my son."

"I know." A great calm had come over Call. He let go of his dad. Somewhere someone was muttering about having Devoureds in the Hall of Graduates, but nobody was actually moving to do anything about it.

A lot had changed at the Magisterium, Call thought, taking his final step toward the Gate of Balance. There was cheering behind him: Alastair, Gwenda, Jasper, even the Rajavis.

He wasn't going through alone. He had support at his back, and his two best friends on the other side.

He took a deep breath and stepped through.

It was the eye of a tornado. Images from his life flashed all around him — a cave of ice, his old skateboard, the kitchen at Alastair's, the Refectory full of students, Master Rufus lecturing, Aaron and Tamara laughing, Havoc as a puppy zipped into Call's coat. Love for all those things rose up in him, expanded in his chest.

He saw the golden tower fall, Alex on his dragon, Drew dangling Aaron over the chaos monster, Anastasia dying, Master Joseph watching him. But he didn't feel anger. He had bested those things, those people. He had won. The better part of him had won, and there were no memories circling him that weren't his own. There were no memories of Constantine Madden's, no memories that belonged to Maugris. Only memories that belonged to *him*.

He knew now who he really was.

He was Callum Hunt.

The tornado whirled away, and the calm that came after it was almost deafening. He was standing on the other side of the gate with Aaron and Tamara; both of them were grinning at him. They'd both made it. For the moment, the crowd couldn't see them — though Call could see the mages in the distance, gazing anxiously toward the gate. In a moment the wall of illusion would fall, but for this moment they were together, unseen.

"We did it," said Tamara. She grabbed Aaron's hand in one of hers, and Call's in the other. "We made it, together."

Call and Aaron linked their hands, too.

"And we've got to promise not to be like the other chaos users," Aaron said to Call, gripping his hand tightly. "Not like Maugris. When we're old and it's time for us to die, we're going to go. We're never going to do anything like this ever again."

Call nodded. "No hopping bodies."

"No hopping bodies," Tamara said. "You watch each other. And I'll watch both of you. And if one of you breaks the pact, it's up to the other one of you to stop it — along with me. Understood?"

Aaron smiled and there was something in his gaze, something odd in those eyes that hadn't always belonged to him. "I promise," he said. "I definitely promise. So long as I live, I will never, ever steal another body again."

Call looked steadily into Aaron's eyes. "I promise, too," he said. "From now on, we play by the rules." He smiled at Aaron, pushing down his flicker of doubt. He was a good person now. They were both good people now.

They just had to stay that way.

ABOUT THE AUTHORS

Holly Black and **Cassandra Clare** first met over ten years ago at Holly's first-ever book signing. They have since become good friends, bonding over (among other things) their shared love of fantasy—from the sweeping vistas of *The Lord of the Rings* to the gritty tales of Batman in Gotham City to the classic sword-and-sorcery epics to *Star Wars*. With Magisterium, they decided to team up to write their own story about heroes and villains, good and evil, and being chosen for greatness, whether you like it or not.

Holly is the bestselling author and co-creator of The Spiderwick Chronicles series and won a Newbery Honor for her novel *Doll Bones*. Cassie is the author of bestselling YA series, including The Mortal Instruments, The Infernal Devices, and The Dark Artifices. They both live in Western Massachusetts, about ten minutes away from each other. This is the fifth book in Magisterium, following *The Iron Trial*, *The Copper Gauntlet*, *The Bronze Key*, and *The Silver Mask*.